EVERY THIRD

About the author

Karin Peters was born in Oxford, January 1986. She has lived in the same street all her life with her Swedish mother, British father and older brother. She is a prolific writer, particularly of songs and poems, this is however her first foray into the world of the novel. She is very committed in her church activities

About Highland Books

You are invited to visit our website www.highlandbks.com to learn more or to download our catalogue. We may also from time to time post errata. If you wish to tell us of significant mistakes you are welcome to e-mail us at errata@highlandbks.com.

EVERY THIRD
PERSON

by Karin Peters

Highland Books

First published in 2003 by Highland Books, Two High Pines, Knoll Road, Godalming, Surrey GU7 2EP.

ISBN: 1-897913-66-4

Printed in England by Bookmarque Limited

AUTHOR'S ACKNOWLEDGEMENTS

THIS BOOK HAS BEEN ONE OF THE HARDEST BUT BEST things I have ever done for myself. It has helped me in so many ways you cannot imagine. It has helped me to accept difficult things that have happened, to learn from these things, and to understand them a little more. I hope that you enjoy my book and that maybe it would help you in some way too.

I couldn't have done this without certain people's help and support. So I would like to thank:

My Mum, Dad and my brother Philip
My grandpa David Peters
Britta Murby
Richard Briggs
Jean-Marc Duckert

+ +

Chapter One

I'm so sorry

THE PLAYGROUND SEEMED SO DESOLATE, IT SEEMED SO empty and dull, nearly scary. The wind made the swings move up and down and the seesaw creek. The gentle rain tipper-tapped onto the window, I sat watching the drops run down the window and onto the windowpane. I was in a dreamland, but there was no dream, no dream at all, my mind was blank, and felt like the empty playground. I was not a happy person, and I needed to change, I needed to try and look up, instead of out.

"What are you doing?" my teacher asked.

"Nothing, Miss, nothing," I replied. I was back in the real world now; I remembered what I'd been doing, before I wandered off. I'd been exchanging notes, as I'd found it so hard to concentrate.

"Are you writing notes, let's have a look," she said, picking up the overturned piece of paper lying on my desk.

"No, please!" I said, but she started to read it aloud anyway.

"What's wrong?"

"Nothing."

"Yes there is."

"OK, I'll tell you, I have got ..." She stopped, looked up at me and carefully whispered the next word ... "Cancer."

She stopped reading, and looked at me, the class was silent. She handed meback the piece of paper, as she did this I ran out of the room trying to hold in my tears, but I couldn't. How could Mrs Landport be so horrible, she just read my life out to the class, I didn't want anyone to know, no one, not even Jonna, but she wouldn't stop pestering me, so I thought it'd be best to tell her.

I sat on the floor of the school toilets crying, my hands over my face, and my knees supporting me. What was I going to do, I couldn't exactly face everyone, could I?

The door slid open, and Mrs Landport walked in. Closing the door firmly behind her.

It was silent for about one or two minutes as she sat down on the floor next to me, put her arm around me and said, "I'm sorry." Nothing to it, it was just a sorry, why was she saying sorry anyway? Because I had it, or because she'd read the note? I wasn't sure what to say, so I didn't.

I just sat crying, and about two minutes later said, "Help me." She looked at me and I looked at her. It was the first time I'd ever seen a nice side to Mrs Landport, she was always so angry and annoyed at me, but it was different now, she seemed so motherly and caring. I just hugged her. It felt so **good**, knowing someone cared, and I know people can't care if they don't know, but it was the telling them that was so difficult.

"Do you want to come back to class?" she asked me.

"No thanks, I think I'll just sit here."

"OK, but do you want me to get Jonna for you?"

"No, no…no thanks," I said, rushed.

"Is it OK if I leave then?"

"Yeah," I replied.

She stood up, didn't turn back, just went towards the door. "Wait," I called. She turned around. "Thank you," I said. She smiled at me, and did a small sort of laugh.

"Any time, you know where I am, OK?"

"Yes." And at that she left.

I knew I had to face up to everybody sometime, so I thought it might as well be now. It was break, and I'd promised Marjorie I'd lend her some money. So I got up off the floor and went to the hall. I felt hot, and red, but I wasn't. I'd checked before I'd left the toilet for tear marks, I must have just been nervous.

I spotted Marjorie, so I walked over, pulling my hand out of my jeans pocket and handed her 25 pence.

"Thank you," she said. She's not in my history class, so doesn't know about what had happened, unless she'd heard from someone.

"You're welcome," I replied.

"Are you OK?" she asked.

"Fine. Why do you think otherwise?"

"Oh, it's just you look like you have been crying," she said.

"No, I'm just tired."

"Cool." She smiled.

I could see Jonna coming towards me, but instead I started towards her, as I didn't want to discuss what had happened in public.

"Hi," she said. We were in the cloakrooms now. She sat down on the bench; I sat down opposite her.

"Hi," I replied.

"I'm so sorry." She started to cry, I got up and hugged her. "How serious is it?" she asked.

"It's quite bad," I said, trying to sound strong.

"How long have you known?"

"I've had it for a year or so, but have only known for a couple of months, but it kept on getting better and then worse again, so I didn't want to say anything unless I was wrong."

"Thank you," she said.

"For what?"

"For telling me. I'm here for you all the way, OK?"

"Thanks. You won't tell anyone, will you?"

"Of course not, not unless you want me to," she replied.

"No, I just want this to be between you and me."

"OK, but half the class know."

"Yeah?"

"Well, what are you going to do about that?"

"I don't know, I think I just won't bring it up and hope they forget."

"Fair enough, but they might talk, you know, twist the tale."

"I know, but all I can do is ignore it," I said.

"I'm with you on that one."

"Thanks, but we'd better go, it's maths!"

"Oh joy!" she huffed sarcastically.

"You're telling me," I agreed.

"See ya!"

I was really quite surprised how nice everyone was … No one was so mean as to spread anything, or at least so I think. Miss must have told them to keep it to themselves or something; otherwise it would be all the way around school by now.

Jonna and Mrs Landport have been great, Mrs Landport in particular, she has just been there, like an extra mother. I am not saying that Jonna hasn't been great, because she has, just not in the same way, it was almost like I had to comfort *her* and help *her*, and isn't it meant to be the other way around? She asks so many questions; most, which I don't even know the answers to myself.

But Mrs Landport was just there, she knew when I was sad, and would just hug me and tell me that everything would be OK … I felt so much better, I really did, it was like she really understood me, and not just understood like any old person, she *really* understood. Sometimes I even wonder whether she had gone through the same sort of thing, I mean she seemed to know exactly how I felt. Sometimes all one needs when one feels sad is a hug, not a load of questions, just a hug … A hug can mean a lot, and that is exactly what it did.

I usually walk home alone, down the main road, into a small cycle path, then a left turn, and my house is on the right. But today was different. I'd left school and was halfway down the main road when this guy Sam came running up from behind me.

"Hiya" he said, a little breathless. Sam is a guy from school, he's in my year and class (i.e. History). I'd never really spoken to him before, I mean he's in the popular gang, who I don't really talk to, and when I do, it is only to respond to something mean they just said to me.

But today was different.

"Hi," I replied.

"How are you?" he asked.

"Fine … I suppose," I replied, a little stunned. "Since when have you wanted to talk to me?"

"Since whenever, I just wanted to say 'Hi'."

"Yeah, I figured, but why?"

"Can't I say 'Hi' without you being shocked and criticising me?"

"You've never wanted to talk to me before. Why now? I don't want sympathy, if that's what you think!"

"I'm just trying to be friendly, but in future I won't." He started off quickly, and did not look back.

"No, wait," I said.

"What?" He stopped and turned around.

"I'm sorry, it's just I didn't exactly plan having the whole class know about my illness."

"I know, it can't be easy, I'm sorry, but I honestly don't just want to talk to you because you are unwell, I wanted to apologise that I haven't been very nice, and I was hoping we could be friends."

"You're kidding, right?"

"No."

"Thank you," I said, stunned.

"You're welcome," he said, and I carried on walking, with him at my side.

I live in a small house, on the corner of Sunnfield Avenue. It's a nice street; it's one of those streets where everyone knows everyone. I've got a couple of friends on it, but not many.

When I got home I went straight to my bedroom, my parents were both out at work, and my brother was at his girlfriend's. I wasn't hungry, so just decided to go upstairs.

I sat down at my desk, put on a little Lauren Hill … and just sat there; did nothing, just sat there, thinking of — don't know, really, I suppose I had a lot to think about. So I took out my diary and started to write a little:

> Dear Diary,
>
> Today wasn't great, everyone found out that I have got cancer … You wanna know how? Mrs Landport read out a note (I'd written to Jonna) to the class … How tight can you get? But it's weird because Mrs Landport's been wonderful … better than anyone has, she

totally understands, and has been really good, it's great, but I still wish that my class didn't know.

You'll never guess who came running up to me after school. Sam, you know, Sam from the popular gang, he just started to talk to me, he knows I have cancer, and I thought he was just talking to me because of it but actually he was just being friendly, but I still reckon that's what triggered him to come and talk to me. He's really sweet, quite fit too, but I'm not saying I fancy him, I barely know the guy ... YET!

See ya, Vada.

I closed my diary and placed it under my pillow ... I'm not quite sure why I put it there, it's not like anyone in my family would read it, it's just I feel happy knowing it's there. It's like putting something difficult away, for the pillow to resolve and take care of, and I suppose that's what my diary was, a load of questions, with no answers.

To be honest I'm scared, what if I don't get through this cancer, I don't want to die, I really don't. What I find so hard is that everyone expects me to be so brave, but it's really hard, it's really hard.

"Hi," my Mum called, "I'm home."

"Hi," I shouted back. I ran down the stairs to see her.

Me and my Mum are like best friends, I tell her everything, and I mean *everything* … anything from guys to just plain old life. And she always seems to be able to help. I love her so much.

"How was your day?" she asked.

"Interesting," I replied.

"What do you mean?"

"My whole class found out I've got cancer, Mum, including Mrs Landport." At this point I burst into tears. She came over and hugged me (there it goes again, a hug can be all you need to make you feel tons better.)

"How?" she asked.

"I was writing a note to Jonna, telling her, and Mrs Landport found out, and without realising read it out to the class," I explained.

"Oh Vada," she said, "what did people say?"

"Nothing," I said. "You'll never believe though … ," and I explained to her about Sam. My Mum was a bit like a diary, come to think of it. She'd be my page to tell things to, and the page helps, just by letting you off-load your problems or worries onto it.

Today was Thursday, which was the day I go to the hospital for a check up. My doctor is Dr Roads. He's very nice, very reassuring, sometimes nearly too reassuring.

"Ready to go?" Mum shouted.

"Yeah, just coming," I said, running down the stairs … going outside and getting into the car. The hospital was about 25 minutes away, it wasn't the normal hospital, it is a special hospital for lung cancer patients … It is even worse than a normal hospital, by the smell and feel of it, I mean. You'd know as soon as you step inside the building that there were people you'd pass in there who'd got cancer like you … but it's how many times you'll be passing them, which I'd always be asking myself.

My name was called and I got up out of my chair, placed the 'SHE' magazine on the table, and followed my Mum into Dr Roads' office. His office was small, but open. His desk was at the back, by the window; to your left was a bookshelf, and two chairs for us to sit on. To your right was a filing cabinet, a notice board and a small cupboard. I'd always wonder what was in that cupboard, I'd had a dream once, all black, but then at the back of my dream was his cupboard, and out of it I came. But I didn't become bigger while walking forwards, it was like I couldn't, like I was never going to get out of the black hole … and was never going to get better.

"How are you doing?" Dr Roads asked, smiling.

"OK, I suppose."

"Well, there's been some good news, we've got your results back and it seems like your tumour is shrinking. But we can't get too chuffed yet, as tumours can often do this, and then stop shrinking, and grow again. But it's a sign that you are definitely on the mend." Dr Roads had a tendency to explain things to me very well, I really liked that, as sometimes I got quite scared going to the hospital, and would just switch off, so I really liked it, that he made everything so clear to me. It was great.

"So you think I'm going to be OK?"

"Well, let's not get too excited yet, it's only been two months."

What did he mean by that? That there was tons left? Oh well, I suppose it's just one of those comments, but I suppose it's quite true.

We talked for about 15 minutes – well, my Mum did a lot of the talking, but I talked a little too. We talked as positively as we could, and tried to keep away from the subject of me having any treatment, even though I knew I'd have to one day. That was something I feared most … losing my hair.

"Well, that went better, did it not?" Mum asked.

"I suppose," I said, and Mum moved forward, and held me tight for several minutes.

I went to school a bit later that afternoon, Jonna and Mrs Landport were the only ones who'd known where I had been, and asked how it had gone.

I don't really like to say much because each week the doctor says something else. One week it's "your tumour is growing," the next week, "it's shrinking". And then the next week it's, "you're on the mend, but just don't get too hopeful yet". It is so annoying, I mean it always changes, I don't really say to anyone what he has said this week, as the next, it will have changed. And then I would have to explain that I was worse again, and I wasn't very good at doing that. So I usually just say that it went OK.

When I got home after school, I made myself a snack, sat down in the living room, and saw some telly, and then Jonna called.

"Hi," she said, "howz life with Vada?"

"Fine, I'm tired, but fine."

"Cool, … what are you doing tomorrow?" she asked.

"Not much, why?"

"Do you wanna come and stay the night?"

"Yeah, sure … " I said.

"Cool, what do you wanna do?" She asked.

"I don't know … we could hire a film or something like that?"

"Great, I will see you tomorrow then."

"OK, see ya," I said, ending that call.

I wasn't sure why I was so nervous, but I was. I suppose I was just nervous of how it would be, as I hadn't talked to her much, and I hadn't stayed the night at her's since she had found out about my cancer. I hoped it wouldn't be awkward.

Chapter Two

For all who love me

I RANG THE BELL, AND JONNA'S MUM CAME TO THE door.

"Ah, hi Vada, how are you?" she asked kindly.

"Fine, umm, Jonna should be expecting me."

"Yes, of course … I'll just call her … come on in." But before either of us had time to do anything, Jonna came running down the stairs, half out of breath, and repeatedly saying "Hi, hi, come on up."

She was smiling so much it was nearly like she had slept with a coat hanger in her mouth.

"Why are you looking so happy?" I asked, smiling slightly myself.

"You're going to love me Vada!"

"What, what have you done?!" I sighed.

"Ah! you are so going to love me!"

"Just tell me!" I squealed ... now up in her bedroom.

"You know Matt, well, he fancies you, and wants to go out with you ... How cool is that!?"

Matt is this guy in my class who I had fancied for several months, until last week. I have to be honest and admit that since Sam came up to me, my feelings towards him had started to grow, and I think I fancy him!

"Did you tell him that I liked him?" I asked.

"Well, not exactly. He told me that he liked you, and then I told him that you felt the same way. Aren't you pleased?" she answered, looking a bit worried.

"I am pleased that you tried but ... Actually, thank you."

"So you'll go out with him?"

"Ok," I said unsure.

"Great, I'll call him now."

I didn't want to go out with him, I didn't even fancy him any longer, but I could tell how hard Jonna had tried, so I didn't want to upset her. And telling her the truth would mean that I would have to explain how I liked Sam, which I didn't want anyone to know.

About a year ago, we made a promise to each other that we would never fancy any of the popular gang. Sam was in that gang, and I knew that if I were to tell her, she was bound to kill me. The thing was that Sam was so different, I have to give him some credit, he did come and apologise to me. Plus she had made such an effort to get Matt and me together, that I was nervous of saying I didn't like him anymore. But she should have consulted me before telling him that I'd liked him, but I suppose that she wasn't to know, but she did break our promise! But on the other hand, so had I, just a different promise. But I can't change how I feel. Feelings are feelings for crying out loud; there isn't anything I can do. They are like people, who do what they want, and go their own way in life, and there is nothing you can do to stop them.

"No, please don't call him, I'll just speak to him on Monday, plus I would like to talk to him alone, no offence or anything."

"OK, that's fair enough, but you are pleased, right?"

I nodded, feeling really guilty, what was I going to say to her for the rest of the evening, I mean, come on, all that she is going to want to talk about is Matt!

We had supper, and saw 'Romeo and Juliet'. I love that film, it is so beautiful, I had loved listening to the way the words flowed like poetry, one of my many dreams is to be in a production of 'Romeo and Juliet', I would love to be Juliet…

We talked for ages after that, well, actually, she did most of the talking, but it was OK, she didn't just talk about Matt.

The next morning we went to town, and you'll never believe whom we bumped into? ... Sam. It wasn't as awkward as I had thought it would be, I just smiled at him, hoping Jonna didn't notice. He smiled back at me, it was really cool. I wondered whether he liked me ... Nope! Impossible! I was unfanciable, I mean the only boyfriend I have ever had lasted two weeks at the most, and I was only twelve years old! I get so jealous of the sorts of people who just go from one guy to the next. I don't think I would like to be popular, some popular people are pretty nasty, and look down on others ... I don't think I would like to be someone like that. But some popular people are nice; some are friendly to everyone, like Sam. I also have a friend called Claudia who I have known since first school, she is really popular, but is one of my best friends, she doesn't look down on me because I am not in the in gang. She is really cool.

I didn't buy anything in town other than some cardboard so I could make Mrs Landport a card, as I wanted to thank her for always being there for me. I have always thought that bought cards don't usually have much feeling; I like to make my cards, they are then much more just from me. Because if you think about it, loads of other people get that same card, and then it isn't really that personal, and then you wouldn't feel that special. But when a card is hand-made, it's the only one of its kind.

Anyway, moving on …

When I got home that evening, I wrote a little in my diary, saw some telly and then made the card for Mrs Landport. This is what I wrote:

> Dear Mrs Landport.
>
> I hope that you are well. I am OK; I am coping at least. I want to thank you for your wonderful support. I know it has only been a few days since you found out about me having cancer, but you have been so cool about it all, so THANK YOU!
>
> I don't mean to be rude, but I was wondering whether you had experienced cancer in any way, it's just you seem to really understand, more than anyone, so again … Thanks.
>
> I hope this letter doesn't seem too weird and out of the blue, because I am writing it so suddenly. But thank you, for everything.
>
> Love Vada

On the front of the card I had painted a picture with my acrylic paints, that I had been given by my Mum a little while ago. I loved to paint, abstract mostly. I loved how I could express exactly how I felt, without an explanation or telling people how I felt. I loved the textures, and the colours and the different lines. I loved to pull my fingers across the painting, with my eyes firmly closed, feeling the different textures, and thinking about things they resembled. I sat hoping that I would always be able to do so.

I gave the card to Mrs Landport on the Monday. I gave it to her in history, but asked her not to open it until I had gone. She smiled at me and said 'of course', while placing it carefully in her drawer, closing it firmly, and repeatedly saying 'thank you'.

At break, Sam came up to me and asked me how I was, which was a nice surprise, especially because of what I had been feeling about him lately ... You know?

"Hiya, how are you doing?" he asked.

"Fine, and yourself?" It seemed to be one of those conversations that really wasn't a conversation at all.

"Me, oh, I'm fine ... " Before he could finish, Eddy, Phil, Eric, Samantha, and Louise came running up to us, and crowded around us ...

"What are you doing talking to her?" Eddy said, putting an accent on the 'her'.

When he said this, I just expected Sam to agree, and walk off, but I was really quite wrong.

"I'm just being friendly, unlike you!" Sam answered.

"Oooh ... am I meant to be scared?"

"No," he said, "you're not, but I'm just being friendly, and if you've got a problem with that, I suggest you get lost!"

They all went, talking amongst themselves … Didn't look back. By the way they acted, you'd really think they were scared, you never know, maybe they were.

"Wow," I said. I know it sounds stupid, but I didn't know what else to say. "Thank you."

"For what?" he replied.

"For sticking up for me … "

"You're welcome," he said. "I'm not scared of them, anyway they're horrible!" I just smiled.

"Can I call you some time?" he asked.

What did that mean? But I answered anyway.

"Sure."

He got out a piece of paper and wrote my phone number out.

"Cheers," he said. "Are you in tonight?"

"Yes … "

"OK, I'll call you tonight, yeah?"

"Sure," I replied.

"See ya," he said.

"Bye!" I said back. And I went to find Jonna.

I had to tell her, I *had* to, this was too big, anyway, did he count as a popular guy now? I don't think so! I decided I was going to tell her, so I went off to find her.

"There you are," I said to Jonna. "I have been looking for you everywhere." She was in the classroom.

"Well, you've found me now."

"Yep, I need to tell you something."

"What, are you OK?" she asked worriedly.

"Yeah, I'm fine, honest."

"Well, go on then."

"You're gonna be so angry with me, though … "

"Just tell me, I won't be angry."

"Well, you know that promise that we made to each other ages ago, you remember? We promised to not fancy anybody from the popular gang … well, I know you'll never believe it, but I fancy Sam." I paused and then went on, "I'm sorry … but I thought it was best you knew, plus I have been dying to tell you … "

"Oh, Vada, why would I be angry? You can't help the way that you feel for someone, but why him? And what about Matt?"

"Well that's the thing, Sam came and talked to me after school one day and apologised, and today he stuck up for me, while his friends were being tight."

"That's so cool, does he fancy you?"

"I don't know, but he asked for my number and he's calling me tonight."

"But what about Matt?"

" I am sorry, I just don't fancy him."

"So you don't wanna go out with him?"

"I am afraid not"

"Oh, I am such an idiot, I should have talked to you first before I went and told him that you liked him! I am so sorry."

"No, I am sorry."

"No, I am sorry!"

This went on for a little while, but then I just hugged her and said. "Shhh, you were trying to help, just relax, it's OK — OK?!"

"Yeah, OK, thank you for telling me though."

"You're welcome. I'll have to call you after I have talked to him tonight."

"You're telling me. You'll have to fill me in on everything!"

"Of course!"

"What are you gonna do about Matt? Would you like me to talk to him for you?"

"No, its OK, I will talk to him … that's the least I can do."

Everything felt so much better after telling her the truth. I hated it how it was before, I felt like I couldn't talk to her about things that were really important. But I suppose she and I both needed a little time to get used to the idea of me having cancer … But luckily the dust was slowly settling.

I spoke to Matt later that morning, and explained why I couldn't go out with him. It went OK, even though he looked really hurt. It is a shame he hadn't told me earlier that he liked me…because I could have then actually been with him for a while … You know … before I started to like Sam. I felt a lot better knowing that he knew, anyway it was important that he knew the truth, otherwise he'd end up being more hurt than now.

After school, I stopped in our nearest newsagent … Lots of people from school were in there, many that were just plain troublemakers … so I just ignored them. I bought a magazine, a Diet *Coke* and a packet of (*Orbit*) gum. While I walked home I flicked slowly through my magazine, carefully noticing every heading. I stopped as I came to one of the headings. It was about cancer, so I read out the heading to myself: "Could you have cancer?" I closed the magazine firmly (not that you could with a magazine), rolled it up in my hand and thought to myself how horrible a title it was. I mean everyone who reads the magazine would get really worried, even if they just read the title! They are not the ones who have to worry; they aren't landed with it! What in the world do the writers of this magazine know about how it is to have cancer … hmm? I am the one who should be worrying; I *am* the one who is worrying!

Every time I think about how I could die, I just want to curl up and cry until there aren't any tears left to cry with. The thought of leaving everything I love, the thought of leaving everything around me, just simple things … everything that we take for granted, the grass, the trees, just simple things like that. Whoever made all these things (and I am not going to even try and go into that now) put a lot of effort into it all, and we just ignore it … (apart from the few tree lovers there are!). We shouldn't ignore these things. Think of all those people who cannot even see the grass, as they sit on it at break. Think of all the people who cannot even feel the grass, who cannot hear the birds sing in the morning … And those who cannot even be here anymore.

From then on I remembered how amazing all of the things around me were. When I sat on the grassy field at break, I didn't complain about how I might get a grass stain, I just sat there, running my fingers through the grass … And listening to the birds sing out their little hearts. I just hoped that I would never have to leave it.

When I got home I sat down at my desk, pulled out my diary and started to write.

Dear Diary,
Today was pretty cool really. Sam came and talked to me at break. His friends took the

mickey out of him and me, and you'll never believe what he did. He stuck up for me. It was really cool. He asked me for my phone number and everything. He is gonna call me tonight, how cool is that? I certainly think that's cool!

I gave a card that I had made to Mrs Landport, and she was really cool about it.

Later this afternoon I bought a magazine, which wasn't a great move. I was flicking through it, when I came across an article on cancer; the title was 'Could you have cancer'. I wanted to just cry when I saw this, I mean it's not a very comfortable thought for all those people who read it. Plus they don't have anything to worry about, do they? I am the one worrying.

I am going to try not to take things for granted, as there is so much to be grateful for ... wish me luck, and I will let you know how I go.

See Ya, Vada

I closed my diary and again placed it underneath my pillow. I got up out of my chair and went to talk to Mum. She was in the kitchen, getting dinner prepared. I offered to lay the table.

"Yes please." She said.

"Mum?" I said, taking the knives and forks out of the drawer, counting carefully. "I'm scared."

"Vada, my dear, of what?" she asked me, placing the wooden spoon down onto the kitchen surface by the stove, and coming forward to me.

"A lot," I answered … "What if I die?"

"Oh Vada, Vada, come here," she said, and I moved forward, clutching the cutlery. She hugged me. "Honey, you won't, you won't … you have to believe in that."

"But what if I do? … Do you reckon there is a heaven? Or do you think I will just lie in a coffin?"

"No, I think there is a heaven, … I do, Vada"

"What do you think it is like?"

"I think it is beautiful. And no one is ever hurt or upset … Everyone is really happy."

"Do you wanna know what I reckon it is like?"

"What?" We were now sitting down.

"I reckon everyone is an angel, and all the angels have one person on earth that they watch over. I think that everyone is happy all of the time and no one is sick or tired. I reckon it is exactly how it sounds … heaven," I explained.

"That is wonderful Vada. Whatever people say to you, believe in that, because I think you are right."

"Thank you Mum. I hope that I don't die. But if I do, then I don't have to be too scared, do I?"

"Yes, you're right … Oh, and Vada," she said as I was turning away, "I love you".

"Same," I agreed.

✹ ✹ ✹

Later that evening, after supper, I was sitting on my bed, and I just couldn't stop crying. I really couldn't, my tears were flowing like a river that wouldn't stop. I cried silently to myself, but then I shouted. I shouted so loudly. I was shouting at God.

"What did I do?!" At that point Mum came running into my room from downstairs. It was 8:32pm, or so my clock said, she had been watching some wildlife programme with Dad.

"What is it, Vada?" she asked, worried.

"I didn't do anything to deserve this!" I screamed.

"It's not about deserving something, it is just something unfortunate that happens, you can't help it, there is nothing you can do. Sometimes God can't even help things, but he can help you fight, he can be there for you and that is what you have to try and do, fight it!"

"But I just don't get it, Mum … " My tears were still flowing, but I had calmed down a little now. "I mean, I don't deserve to die, do I? I don't even deserve to be ill. I'm only 15 years old. I am so scared, and for some reason it has just hit me now, how scared I really am."

"Come here," Mum said, and I got up out of my desk chair and hugged her. I didn't want to ever let go. If I were to have a favourite place, this would be it, in my Mum's arms. I feel safe there, I feel like myself.

After a good talk with Mum, Sam called me, at about 9:00pm. We talked for ages, about tons of stuff, but mostly about his friends. He said something really nice, he said that whatever happened, he was there for me. I know that that's what everyone says, but it was different coming from the guy you fancy, from the guy you dream about all day and night, and from the guy that you long to just hold. It was nicely different. I rang Jonna straight after, even though it was quite late. I told her all about him and the conversations we had had. But I missed out all the things we had said about cancer to each other. I just didn't feel like I could talk to Jonna about it, as I was worried that she would take it the wrong way, you know?

I got to sleep around 12:20 that night, after another good talk with Mum.

I left for school at 8:20, a little late, but I got there just in time. I put my coat in my locker, then I went to registration. I sit next to a guy called Andrew. He's so quiet, he never talks to me. I don't mind, but I always wonder whether he's OK, but I suppose you can be quiet without being upset.

I didn't have history today, so I wasn't expecting a letter back from Mrs Landport, but then Miss Webb (my form tutor) asked me up to the front.

"Yes … ?" I said.

"This is for you." She handed me an envelope with. It wasn't money, and it didn't look like a letter to my parents, so I went back to my seat, and opened the envelope. No one was looking at me. So I pulled out the card and read it to myself:

> Dear Vada,
>
> Thank you for the beautiful card and letter. I love your painting.
>
> I am glad you feel I can help you, and am there for you, because I am, I always am, you know where to find me.
>
> You asked me whether I'd experienced cancer in any way, and the answer is yes, I have. Last year my daughter, Catherine, died of cancer, she was very brave, like you ... I only just got through it, with help though. I think that if I hadn't have told anyone, then I would have found it harder to cope. I haven't told anyone in school about this, so I'd be grateful if you could keep it to yourself.
>
> Thank you, and take care.
>
> Marianne Landport

After I'd read this letter, I realised something that I should have realised a long time ago ... how difficult this is and will be, if I die, for my Mum.

The day went quite quickly really. Jonna was in a bit of a mood. I'm not quite sure why, though. But later that afternoon I asked her.

"What's wrong?"

"Nothing," she grunted.

"Stop playing around 'cause it's obvious there's something wrong, so you might as well tell me," I said.

"It's just … " she paused.

"Go on," I said.

"It's just … oh I can't say. You'll get really offended."

"I won't, OK?"

"Look … It's like this. I just feel like you are getting loads of attention from other people, and then don't wanna talk to me, and don't wanna be my friend any more."

"Oh Jonna, that's not true!" I paused and thought about what to say next. "It's just I don't feel I can talk to you about 'everything', so I talk to others about it, but that certainly doesn't mean I don't like you, because I do. A lot. You're a great friend, and I love you dearly."

"Thank you … ," she said, "but you do know I am here, not just because of your … You know." She looked at me.

"Cancer," I said. Why can't she just say it? I mean, it's so annoying. Does she think I can't handle it or something?

"Yes, that's right, I am here for you in everything else too, OK?"

"Thanks."

We were silent for a moment, then I moved forward and hugged her.

Later that evening I spoke to Mum. I spoke to her about what I'd been feeling earlier, about how it all is for her.

"It must be hard for you, too," I added, after our conversation had been going for a little.

"Darling, please don't feel guilty, because you have no need to at all, OK?"

"OK, but it still must be hard for you."

"I find it tough, but I believe that together we can fight it …"

"It's hard to fight something I can't control, though," I pointed out.

"Yes, it is. But we can try and fight it, as even just trying will help."

"Thank you *so* much … !" I shouted.

"Vada, don't get angry now."

"Trying. Trying. What in the world do you think I'm TRYING TO DO?!!"

"Vada, calm down. You know that's not what I meant"

There was a small pause and I thought about what I'd said.

"I'm sorry … I just find it all really hard to accept … but that's no reason to take it out on you. I'm sorry."

"Don't worry, Vada. I understand. And I know you're trying. All I'm saying is never stop trying, as trying can help a lot." Mum smiled and kissed me on my cheek.

"Thanks," I said. "I'll be in my room if you want me."

Before I had time to leave, the phone rang.

"Hello," my Mum said, picking up the phone.

"Hi, it's Sam here. Is Vada in?"

"Yes, hold on a moment." She put her hand over the mouthpiece and whispered to me, "Honey, it's SAM," saying 'Sam' in a sort of exaggerated way. She smiled and handed me the phone.

"Hi."

"Hi," he answered.

"Hold on one sec, I'm just gonna go to the upstairs phone."

"OK," he said.

As I was walking up the stairs I was thinking about Sam. I was thinking about how and who he really was; where did he spring from; and why did he take an interest in me, not necessarily as a girlfriend but just a friend. He's so nice. He's so open and caring. I know it sounds weird, but he's like the bestest 'girl' friend I could ever have, not the sort of friend that I could talk to about really girlie stuff, but someone I can really confide in. Or maybe it's just that I am not used to having a guy friend. I dunno. It's just that Jonna can get so annoyed with me for things I point out. I want to be able to say anything without being told off, or feeling guilty, and for some reason I can do that with Sam. I suppose I shouldn't judge too much yet, as I barely know him yet. But what I do know … I LIKE!

"Hi, sorry about that."

"Don't worry," he said in a sort of *Drew-from-Neighbours-type* way.

"So, how are you?" I asked.

"Not too bad, thanks."

"You?" he asked.

"Ok … Well, actually, I'm a bit worse."

"I'm sorry," he said.

We talked for ages, but just before we said goodbye, he said something that really shocked me. Or maybe not.

"What would you say if I were to ask you out?" There was a long pause and he said, "Oh, please say something."

"Yes. I believe I'd say yes."

"You would?"

"Yeah."

"I'll see you tomorrow then … "

"Ok … Goodnight," I smiled.

"Goodnight."

I lowered the phone slowly from my ear, paused, and then I turned it off. I had to come to terms with what I'd just done. For crying out loud, I'm going out with SAM! I am sooo pleased, but a little nervous. I mean, he's quite popular. What in the world will people think? I'm really happy, though.

I ran downstairs to tell Mum.

"You'll never believe it, Mum," I said, out of breath.

"What?" she asked.

"I'm going out with Sam! … How cool is that?"

"Oh, Vada, I'm so happy for you!" she smiled.

"What? … " I asked, as I thought it was weird how she was so quiet and looked a little sad.

"It's just … You're growing up, and … ?"

"I know. I'm sorry … " I hugged her.

Even though that was all she said, I knew what she felt. I knew that she was thinking, 'What if she dies? Sam will also be sad.' Well, I've thought of that, and well, hey, he wouldn't ask me out if he didn't feel he could cope, would he? Now I'm even more nervous! I'll talk to him tomorrow …

Remember how I said I was a bit worse? Well … It's true, I am. I am feeling very weak. I can just tell … but it's OK. It's soon Thursday, and I can talk to Dr Roads about it, though I just want to ignore it and hope it'll all go away by itself. But I have to remember what Mum said. I can't stop trying!

I was going to call Jonna last night to tell her what had happened with Sam, but I decided I'd wait till the morning as I was very tired, and just didn't feel up to talking to her. But when I woke up, I could barely move I was feeling so weak and unwell. My Mum came in and felt my forehead. "You don't seem to have a temperature, Vada."

"Of course I don't have a temperature, Mum. It's my cancer. That's why I feel like this."

"Oh Vada … Don't worry. You had better just stay home today and then we'll talk to Dr Roads. Ok?"

"But I want to go to school. I want to see Sam!" I got up … well, tried to get up, but just collapsed back into my bed. My head hit my pillow, like a baby being dropped and hitting the floor with a thud. My head was now thumping and really hurt.

"Ok, maybe not … " I said. "I just didn't realise that the cancer would make me feel like this."

"I know, Vada, it's very difficult, but you are bound to feel like this now and again," she said, and went on. "Vada, we need to talk to Dr Roads about how long this is going to go on for. And maybe if there is anything we can do to make you feel remotely better."

I stayed home through the whole day, but I didn't want to. I wanted to go to school and see Sam. I wanted to see Sam …

That afternoon he called me. He must have only just got back from school as it was 4.05 when he called and school finishes at 3.45 p.m.

"Are you OK?" he asked, sounding a little worried.

"Nooo, I'm not. I'm feeling really sick and weak," I explained.

"So it wasn't because of me you didn't come to school?" he asked.

"Of course not. I've wanted to see you all day, and have been thinking of you constantly. It's not you, I promise."

"Is it the cancer?" he asked nervously.

"Yes, we think so."

"I'm sorry," he said reassuringly.

"Well, it's just lucky I have got an appointment with my doctor tomorrow."

There was a small pause.

"Does the school know about your cancer?"

"No, but they probably will find out from Mum as she'll have to explain why I wasn't in school today."

"I suppose," he said. "I'm sorry to be short but I really have to go."

"No problem," I said. "Nice to talk to you."

"Will you be in school tomorrow?"

"I hope so," I answered. "See ya."

"Bye."

I put the phone down, and sat there for a moment. Then just burst into tears.

I know it sounds silly, but it helps to cry. It helps to let it all out … you know?

"Ready," I heard Mum shout.

"Coming," I said as we left the house to go to Dr Roads.

Dear Diary,

The appointment went OK, I suppose. Dr Roads explained that I would often feel like this and there wasn't much he could do about it. But he told me to keep positive and eat and be healthy. Easy to say, but when you feel tired and weak, it's a little difficult to do exercise! Just before we were about to leave he said that the tumour was growing again and that chemotherapy had to be a possibility. He just threw this at us, but why all at once, at the end of the appointment too? Did he think it wouldn't hurt as much if he told us then, or was it because he didn't want to talk about it? I don't know, I really don't.

... Chemotherapy; you've got to be kidding, right? Losing my hair is just out of the question!

Vada

I told Sam later that day what the doctor had said. I didn't go to school as I just felt too sick and weak.

"I might have to have chemotherapy," I told him. "I don't want to lose my hair."

"Isn't it worth it, if it were to help you get better?" That was the first thing he'd said to go against me ... Not exactly go against me, but just look at another side of things. But, come to think of it, I hadn't looked at it like that before ...

"Of course I want to get better!" I started to cry ... And explained I had to go.

"I didn't mean it like that."

"Oh, I know. I know. I'm not angry. It's just I'm really tired."

"No probs. I'll see ya soon, then."

"Ok. See ya."

"Bye."

Chemotherapy. Chemotherapy. The word rang in my ears constantly all day and all night. I got no sleep at all!

The next day I felt so sick, I even had difficulties breathing. But then something unexpected happened.

I collapsed … I was walking to the toilet and just collapsed onto the bathroom floor. It was horrible. I just faded out … my mind went blank. But for the first time I had a NICE dream. It was about fields and fields of flowers, and Sam and I were sitting amongst them, and he picked some for me.

The only next thing I can remember is waking up in a hospital bed … Mum, Dad and my brother sitting at my side. You should have seen the look on their faces when my eyes flickered open. Mum was as white as a sheet, and Dad was a little red. But Nick, my brother, was just normal … I liked that.

"Vada, Vada, are you awake? Can you hear me?" Mum said, getting out of her chair and coming towards me.

"Huh, where am I?" That was all I managed to say. How imaginative. I always heard people say it on Soaps or TV series, but I never thought I'd be saying it. It just seemed far too corny

"You're in hospital, Vada. You collapsed on the way to the bathroom," Dad explained. "But you're OK," he reassured me.

I could see Nick sitting by my feet, with his hand gently placed on my foot … he smiled at me and said the sweetest and nicest thing I think I've ever heard him say, "I'm here for you, and I'll always love you."

"I love you too, Nick," I said back.

I closed my eyes again and just lay there. I didn't sleep. I just lay there … I could hear voices all around me, doctors, nurses and my family … reassuring voices, until I heard Mum say,

"So, it's getting worse … " I assumed IT was the cancer.

"I'm afraid so," I heard some sort of medical person say.

Then my brother asked THE question.

"Will she die?"

"It's too early to say yet, but if she doesn't do the chemotherapy, she may get a lot worse."

There was a silence. Well, not by them as they were still talking. But there was with me as I switched off. I didn't want to hear any more.

When I woke up the next morning, I noticed Mum's face staring down at me, it was the first thing I saw.

"Hi," I managed to say.

"Vada, Vada, it is so good you're awake."

"Why, what's happened?".

"You're ill Vada, very ill, and to get better, we need you to agree to do some sort of treatment, possibly chemotherapy." I started to cry, even though I knew this already, it hurt so much to hear it, to hear that I was really really ill. And if I was to feel even remotely better, it was I who had to take the first step.

"Are you OK?"

I sniffed and then hugged her, with the little strength I had left. "Yep, OK. I will try something." Mum told me how the doctors were pretty worried about my condition. She told me that I could die, but that they were all trying not to be too negative yet. But the thing was, I wanted to know the truth even if the truth hurt, I wanted to know.

I slept for the rest of the day, well I didn't sleep, I just rested. I had so much pain, that I couldn't eat, or even do the simplest thing … to sit up. Going to the toilet is a difficulty, for crying out loud … and that's why I'm here in the first place!

I have a pain, a pain I really can't explain, the only way to explain it is that it's a nasty pain, a pain I want to get rid of.

The next morning, Sam was sitting by my bed.

"Sam," I smiled. I wondered how he knew I was here, Mum must have told him or something.

"Vada! … How are you feeling?" He was red in the face and had blood-shot eyes.

"Not very well—I'm sorry, I'm so sorry." I started to cry, but tried desperately to hold in my tears. I didn't want to cry in front of him.

"Sorry? For what?"

"You're going out with me, and I'm here, I'm in a hospital bed, and I might be dying of cancer."

"I want to go out with you, whatever, whether you're a millionaire, or whether you are ill, I still want to be your boyfriend, nothing will change that, unless you don't want to be my girlfriend."

"Of course I want to be your girlfriend, I need you."

"I need you too, but I'm here for you, whenever, whatever."

"Thanks." He came over and kissed me, that was our first kiss, and I can't say I expected it to be in a hospital bed.

Later that day, Dr Roads came to visit me. You see he doesn't work in the hospital, he works in a cancer clinic a few miles away from here. It was nice to see him, as his face was one of those faces that was very comforting and reassuring, I liked that. I know it sounds silly and like I'm a five-year-old, but some of the other doctors scare me a bit. I've always associated doctors with 'helping others' and 'curing', but then on the other hand, I associate them with 'death', as they are the people who bring the bad news, whether it's when your Grandma or Grandpa dies, or whether it's you yourself who is critically ill.

"Ahh, Vada, " he smiled. "I've heard that you've had a little bit of a difficult time … "

"Yep." I know that sounds silly, but it was all I could think of to say.

"Is treatment out of the question?"

"No … it's not … I just … I don't want to lose my hair, or feel worse, but before you say anything, I also want to get better, so … maybe … "

"The treatment would help a lot, and I know it'll be hard, but it would be good if you could get better in the long term too … yes?"

"Yes."

"I'll speak to the doctors and your parents about it, I'll see you soon, OK?"

"OK, see ya."

When he'd left, I couldn't hold in my tears, I burst out crying, and Mum came rushing in.

"What is it? What is it?" she said in a worry.

"I don't want to have treatment, but I want to get better, I want to go to school and see Mrs Landport and my friends! I don't want to be ill, Mum, I don't want to!"

"Vada, shhhh," she said, holding me. I sat up, and she was at my side, on my bed, holding me, "Shhh … shhh … You'll get better Vada, it'll just take time and effort."

"I'm trying … I'm trying!"

"I know, but you need to do some sort of treatment, it would help, it would help."

"But I don't want to lose my hair, and look like a bald person, I don't want to."

"Not everyone loses their hair, you know, and that's not the only worry here!"

"I know, but I might."

I'd calmed down a little now, but I felt sick, I had a pain and it just wouldn't go away, it's like one of those everlasting headaches!

"OK, I'll do it. I'll do the treatment."

"Oh, Vada. You'll be better in no time at all!" She hugged me, and even started to cry, not that I blame her!

I couldn't sleep that night. My mind was spinning with images and questions. Other people in the ward weren't sleeping either. Some would just constantly cough, others just cried and cried, while others just screamed. All muffled sounds, but they kept me awake, those people were in pain too, and that made it all much more difficult to accept.

I was in a large ward, each bed separate, with a curtain around it, so I was a little closed in, but I liked that, as I'd hate for everyone to see me, all the time.

The next morning Mum and Dad came to see me, and you'll never believe who they brought, Mrs Landport. I was shocked, but very pleased, Mum and Dad left us alone for a while.

"Vada, long time no see," she said. "I've missed you a lot, I think about you often."

"Same, it's so nice to see you!"

She started to cry, I couldn't say I'd often seen a teacher cry.

"Are you OK?" I asked, manoeuvring my hand over to hers.

"I'm fine, I just remember sitting here, by a hospital bed, when my daughter was ill."

"I'm sorry, you don't have to be here if you don't want to be."

"I want to be here, I wanted to see you."

There was a pause, while she dabbed her eyes with a tissue, 'trying' to wipe away her tears.

"Do you think I'll be OK?" I asked.

"Yes, yes I do."

"But I'm scared to take treatment."

"It'll make you better, Vada."

"I know, so people keep on telling me."

"You'll be fine," she reassured me.

We talked for ages, about school, and a little about her daughter. Just before she got up to leave, she pulled out an envelope from her bag. It was a large red envelope. She handed it to me.

"Wait until I've gone to open it," she said.

"OK. Will I see you soon again?"

"I'll come soon and visit you again, next week maybe, I'll call your Mum to arrange something, OK?"

"Yes, oh and Miss, … thanks!"

"You're welcome! See you soon." She pulled the grey and red curtain back, stepped out of my cubicle, and closed the curtain behind her.

As soon as she'd left, I opened the envelope. Inside lay a large card, and I took it out of its envelope and turned it over to look at the front. On it was a collage of lots of pictures, teddies, hearts, stars, beds, and people, it was beautiful. Inside was this message:

> Dearest Vada,
>
> We are all thinking of you, and hope you will soon get better.
>
> Take care.
>
> Your class.

Everyone from my class had signed it, and some others, it must have even been around the staff-room, as most teachers had signed it too. Each individual person had written something.

It was the most beautiful card I'd ever seen. I felt so touched. They cared, they really did care, and I decided that even if I lose my hair, even if I feel sick and weak, I want to get better, if not for me, then for them, and all the people who love me.

The next day was a Sunday, and you'll never believe who came to visit, my curate and church friends. The curate at my church is the coolest guy ever, he is so nice and friendly. My church friends are the nicest in the whole world, they are true and honest friends, they're the sort of friends I know I could go to with anything, whether it's a good thing or a bad thing. They prayed for me, it was lovely. They prayed that I'd soon get better, and that I could soon come home and go to school and church again. They also prayed that I'd feel God near, that I'd know he was there for me, and actually I needed help with that, as I felt like this was his fault, like he wanted me to be ill! But maybe it wasn't him, maybe he wanted me up there for a reason. But I really did feel like I needed him. I was just hoping that this prayer would help.

Chapter Three

Visits and baby food

A COUPLE OF DAYS HAD PASSED, IT WAS NOW A Wednesday. I hadn't done much in the last few days, other than trying to keep my spirits up, and trying to become a bit stronger. I hadn't been eating much in the last week, so they'd been feeding me through pills, injections and a drip. I felt like a pincushion for crying out loud. They say it makes me feel stronger, and ready for treatment, even though I feel so weak I can barely sit up. On the Wednesday morning Sam came to visit me, he came just before school, as he passes the hospital.

"How are you doing?" he asked me, popping his head through the two drawn curtains.

"Me, I'm feeling weak and tired, but am OK."

"Any more news on the treatment front?"

"Well, Dr Roads and Dr Miles are coming to talk to me tomorrow about the treatment, and when we'll start, and what will happen. Dr Susan Miles is my new doctor at the hospital, unlike Dr Roads who works at the cancer clinic. Dr Miles is really quite nice; she's a bit patronising but she's OK. There's another lady called Marie, who is going to be the lady who helps me through it all, and make sure I feel OK about it all. Dr Roads and Dr Miles will help me do the treatment, you see."

"Gosh, you seem pretty clued up on it all."

"Well, I like to know what's happening to me," I explained.

"I suppose," he agreed. "Well, I better be off, as it's school."

"Sure, but can I just ask? … "

"Go ahead."

"How's everything at school? Anyone asked after me?"

"Didn't you get the card?" he said, sounding surprised.

"I did. But … "

"Well, Jonna and Marjorie are constantly asking me where you are."

"What did you say?"

"I said that you were in hospital, to Jonna, as I know she knows about you."

"What about Marjorie?"

"I said that I didn't know."

"Thanks … Keep it that way, yeah?"

"Sure, that's cool." He got up and kissed me, I kissed back; I'd lifted my arms and placed them on his shoulders. And his were placed on the back of my head. It was the best kiss I'd *ever* had … I could still barely believe it was with Sam!

For the rest of the day I hung about thinking about stuff. Nick came to visit me too, which was nice, as I hadn't seen him for a little while. Nick and me get on quite well really. We have periods when we get on very well, and periods when we constantly argue, but because I'm not well, he's really nice and doesn't want to get me upset, and vice versa. I love Nick loads though. I talk to him about Sam, not too much though, as I'm a bit nervous he'll tell his friends, but he gives quite good advice so I talk to him about stuff quite often … But for some reason today, he didn't say much, so I asked him.

"What's wrong?"

"Nothing, nothing."

"Look, just because I'm ill, doesn't mean everyone else has to be happy and problem-less all the time, you can tell me your problems too. What do you think I'm gonna do? Do you think that I'm going to think that you're trying to get the attention, and make out that your problem is bigger than mine is, and burst into tears? Well, I'm not, I can handle it, you know. To be honest I'd love the attention to be off me for a bit!" I took a breath… and then said, "I'm sorry, I didn't mean to take it all out on you … I'm sorry."

"Don't worry, I understand."

"So what's wrong?"

"I'm scared of losing you. I love you Vada." He closed his eyes and placed his hands over his face and leaned forward.

"I'll be fine, hey," I said, trying to get him to look up at me. "I'll be fine."

He nodded and smiled. "I hope so," he said.

"Anyway, I've got this meeting tomorrow and I'm gonna get everything sorted then, OK?"

"OK!"

That night I slept very badly. I felt sick and had real troubles breathing. I was scared, I was really, really scared. And I just wanted to go home to my warm bed, with my Mum beside me, I wanted it all to go away, I wanted this to never have happened. And I know you think, that's what everyone says, but believe me, there's nothing I want more than to be well again, and be put out of this pain.

In the morning I felt a bit better, but still had pains in my chest and found it hard to breathe properly.

Mum and Dad came at 9:30, as we had the meeting at 10. They wanted to be here for it. I was so nervous, what if the treatment didn't work?

Well, 10 o'clock came and my small section of the ward was filled with Mum, Dad, Dr Miles, Dr Roads and Marie. It was so full that I felt quite claustrophobic, I asked them to open the curtains around us a little. I felt so nervous; you would, if you were stuck in bed with no way of getting out.

"Well, shall we start?" Dr Roads said, looking at me. I nodded, and he proceeded.

"As we all know, Vada is a very poorly girl right now, and we need to work out the best type of treatment for her." I sat in bed, wondering whether he realised I was even there!

"Vada has a type of chest tumour called lymphoma. Normal chest tumours aren't too common in people of Vada's age. But lymphoma is more common. Luckily we've caught this cancer in time so it hasn't spread too much. But we need to get rid of it, and make her feel better and back to normal."

Back to normal? Back to normal? I could barely remember how that felt ... Anyway, what is normal?

Dr Roads went on. "Dr Miles and I have discussed all possibilities of treatment, and have come to the conclusion that chemotherapy is the best. For lymphoma, that's one of the most common treatments. For Vada there were other possibilities, but we've worked out chemotherapy will be best."

"What will it involve?" Mum asked.

"Chemotherapy is a means of treatment by using chemicals and pills such as anti-cancer drugs, which will work over a period of time."

"How long will it last?" Mum asked again.

"It's very different for different people, and it depends on the size of the tumour, but for Vada it will work over a period of about six months or so. She'll come in every month for some treatment, go home, then she'll come back in again after a month or so for some more treatment, and home again … And so on … Chemotherapy can have quite bad side effects, and that's why we spread the treatment out."

"Like what?" I asked worriedly.

"Well again it depends on the person. You may experience some nausea, vomiting, loss of appetite, night sweats, excessive tiredness, indigestion, abdominal pain, bone pain, and maybe loss of hair."

A tear rolled down my cheek. Mum put her hand on mine and squeezed it hard.

"How long will those effects last for?" Mum asked.

"Well, they usually go away after a few days of the treatment."

That meant that I'd have my treatment, come home, feel sick, feel sick, feel sick, then feel better, but then it'd all happen all over again! Yeah? How dumb! I thought to myself, I suppose it's better to go through with it, as I do want to get better.

"You may also have a shortage of breath, due to low blood cell counts, that will probably last for a bit longer, I'm afraid."

"What if I don't feel better?" I asked.

"Well, there are types of medicines such as antiemetic drugs, which can prevent or reduce nausea and vomiting."

"Good," said my Dad. "Are you happy with this, Vada?"

I nodded, I think I was. I was just nervous.

"Good, well … would anyone else like to say anything? Vada, do you have any questions?"

"No," I said. Even though I felt like I did, I didn't, I had non-answerable questions, and thoughts, flying around in my head, but definitely nothing I'd like to share.

"Could I just say something?" Dr Miles said.

"Go ahead," Dr Roads replied.

"I'd just like to say that I think you are being brilliant about this all. It must be very difficult, but your bravery really stands out a lot, Vada, it really stands out."

"Thank you," I said, "I like to think so."

"Hear hear!" Dad said.

Everyone laughed slightly, it was nice, it felt nice to smile. Marie seemed like a very quiet person, she hadn't said anything through the whole meeting. But I was wrong, when everyone left, Marie stayed and she started talking, and I swear it was flowing out of her, I thought she'd never stop. But I didn't mind, she seemed quite nice really.

"You are going to need to keep healthy and strong throughout, and that's what I'm here for. We are going to go swimming weekly, and will do exercises. What other sports do you like doing? We can do them if you like."

"I like basketball."

"Great! There's a basketball club here in the fitness hospital. You can join that, there are lots of girls your age on that team, so you can make some new friends at the same time ... Yes? Does this sound OK?"

"Yep, but you won't leave me, will you?"

"Relax, of course not."

"Thank you very much." I said.

"You're very welcome, and I look forward to getting to know you a bit more ... yes?"

"Yep."

"See ya," she said, getting out of the chair, and leaving.

"See ya!"

Marie was a lady in her mid 20s, she seemed really nice, a bit mad but nice. She was a black lady, with her hair in dreadlocks. She wore combats and a tight T-shirt, with a small cardigan on top. She seemed quite cool really, energetic but cool.

Maybe this wouldn't be too bad after all?!

After Marie had left, Mum and Dad came back in.

"Well, that went well, didn't it?" Dad said, unsurely.

"Yep." I smiled and held out my arms, for them to hug me ... they both came over and we hugged for what felt like ages. It was lovely. For some reason I felt happier, and more positive, I'm gonna get through it, I know I will, I'm gonna be fine ...

For the rest of the day I rested, I was so tired as I hadn't slept well the night before, plus the meeting had sort of tired me out. I had no visitors all day, in a way I was quite pleased, but in another way, I wasn't. I wanted to talk to people, I wanted to see my friends. I really wanted to get better, so I could go to school again, and see all of my friends ... oh, and Mrs Landport, but I suppose she sort of counts as a friend, doesn't she? I hope so anyway.

That night I slept like a log, but I didn't have a nice dream at all. I dreamt the most awful thing possible, I dreamt that I died, because of the chemotherapy. I dreamt it wasn't working, so in the morning I was even more scared to have the treatment. But I knew I had to have it, I knew that I had to get better, but dreams like that didn't help.

When the nurse came in to check on me at 9:00am I was crying. She asked me what was wrong.

"Nothing," I replied

"Yes there is, you can tell me, I won't tell anyone."

"I had a dream, about my treatment. What if it doesn't work and it just makes me feel worse?"

"You'll be fine, try and be positive … and remember, it was just a bad dream … "

"I know, but dreams scare me, especially as I'm not at home, and I'm in this strange building."

"Well, think in a couple of days, once you start eating again, you'll be able to go home." She handed me a plate with some baked beans on toast on it and a glass of orange juice. "Hmmm?" she said, lifting her eyebrows and pushing the plate towards me.

"Maybe just a little," I said. She smiled and got out a serviette, a knife and a fork. "Oh, Julie … Thank you." I said.

"You're welcome." And at that she left.

I managed to eat a little of the baked beans, but the toast was too tough, plus I was worried that I would throw it all up.

Mum came to see me around 10:30am.

"Vada, how are you this morning, darling?"

"OK, Mum," I lied.

"You've eaten something, honey."

"Only a few spoonfuls."

"Well that's a start, well done." I smiled and she went on. "I've got some good news."

"What?"

"The doctor says that you are getting stronger and if you carry on eating a little, then you can come home on Monday."

I thought to myself … 'Well, today was a Friday, then it was the weekend, then Monday, only 3 days away! Yippee!!'

"That's great, Mum!" I leaned forward to hug her.

"But you have to try and eat, otherwise the doctor will reconsider his decision."

"I'll try, I promise." The idea of getting out of this hospital was the best ever. I hated it here, it scared me, I always had bad dreams, and could never sleep properly. I imagined sleeping in my own bed again, the feel of my own duvet, the feel of my own pillow! Heaven!

I know it's something simple, but believe me, once you've been away from it for a while, and you think you'd never be there ever again, you can miss it a lot! I tried to remember when I was last at home … It was when I had been off school for a while as I felt sick and then I'd got up for the toilet and had collapsed. I'm such an idiot, and a fool, I must be a real embarrassment to my family and friends! 'I'm such an idiot!' I thought about those words for a while, but I wasn't a fool, I wasn't an idiot, it wasn't my fault that I was ill with cancer, or was it … ?

That afternoon Sam came to see me. He had come quite a lot before, but I had often been asleep. It was so nice to see him, but you'll never guess who he brought? Well, actually you probably will. He brought Jonna, I spoke to them for ages, until it was 6:30 (they arrived at 5), they caught me up on the gossip and school. Then Sam left so I could talk to Jonna alone a bit. I told her about my treatment and that I might be coming home soon. She seemed pleased, I certainly was, but I just think she finds it difficult to see me like that, you know, a bit pale and weak, but hopefully that was all about to change … Hopefully anyway!

It was such a surprise to see them; it felt a bit weird though, as I was just lying in a bed, sick. And they'd just been at school, working all day, while I'd been lying in bed, thinking, crying and listening to music. But I suppose you could think about anything like that. I'm lying in bed while some lady in a hospital far away is giving birth to a little baby boy and somewhere else, a small child is collecting barrels of water for his family in third world countries … scary or what?

That evening, I tried to eat a little more; I managed some mashed potato with a little sausage. It was baby-food so it went down easily, it wasn't too bad.

The weekend went by slowly, I didn't do much, other than trying to eat a bit more every day and listening to music. My favourite music was 'Lauryn Hill' and 'Travis.' I'd put their albums on repeat, and would just lie in bed, mouthing out the words to myself. By Monday I knew every song on both of the albums off by heart. Mum had brought me some photos on Saturday to cheer me up. They were of me when I was a few years old … I wish I was that age again, life was always so simple. The only thing that would worry me then was if my Dad played with someone else, and now I wouldn't care, now I know what sharing is. It's funny how things change, isn't it?

At last, Monday came, Mum and Dad came in at about 11:00am to talk to the doctors and make sure I was strong enough to leave. They told Mum and Dad that I'd improved, and that I'd been eating better and that I'd been very patient and good all weekend. They said that I deserved to go home. Mum came in to tell me the good news while Dad went to get a coffee. Mum started packing my things up.

"Dr Roads and Dr Miles say that you are doing brilliantly and that you deserve to go home," she said.

"Great!"

"But that doesn't mean you can go back to school yet, you will still have to stay in bed and have lots of rest, but you need to try and get used to walking around and stuff again…"

"I can do that …" I smiled.

"I know you can … I'm not doubting you, I'm merely just passing on what they said."

"When can I go back to school?"

"We'll see Vada, we'll see."

At that, Dr Miles came in and said, "How are you doing in here, set to go home?"

"Getting there … " I replied.

"Good, good."

"When would you like us to come in for Vada's first treatment?" Mum asked.

"Well, if you come to my office before you leave, I'll talk to you about it, OK?"

"Yep," I smiled.

I packed up my things and got dressed in my favourite clothes. My dark blue flared jeans that were so long that they touched the ground. My blue shirt with patterned white stripes on it (three-quarter length sleeve) and my black and blue body-warmer from *Gap*.. It was so nice to put on my favourite clothes and not have to be wearing my stupid nightie anymore. My Mum took my bag with my things in it and I held my jacket and my plastic bag with cards and letters in it. You'd be surprised how many envelopes I'd got, filled with beautiful cards, letters or gifts with pretty ribbons wrapped around them.

I walked through the ward and out of the door, down another corridor and into a small office. It was Dr Miles' office.

"Come on in," she said. "How are we feeling, umm?"

"Not bad thanks, not bad," I said.

"Good, now you were asking when you should come in for your first appointment, and well, I've scheduled you in for next Monday … A week today, how's that?"

"That's great, isn't it Vada?" Mum looked at me and smiled. I nodded, but said nothing.

"Great, I'll expect you next week, OK?"

"Yep." Mum and I got out of our chairs and went towards the door.

"Take care," Dr Miles said as we were just opening the door to leave. She said it in a way that sounded like she really meant it.

"I will," I replied, smiling as I left.

I walked briskly down the corridor, eager to get out of this 'building'. I was wobbly on my feet, as I'd been in bed for so long. My head hurt and my eyes went out of focus now and again as my head was spinning. The moment I stepped outside I felt the cool brisk air smother me, but it wasn't cold, it was just brisk. The sun was shining, in the shade it was cold but in the sun it was lovely … it was lovely!

I was at last out of that 'building' and was leaving to go home, to my house, my room and my bed. In the car there was silence for ages, I didn't know what to say, but then Mum said, "Are you really feeling OK?"

"Umm … I suppose so, but I'm a bit nervous."

"Well Vada, that is to be expected."

There was another silence, then, "Why did you choose to call me Vada?" I asked, intrigued.

"Don't you like your name?"

"I love it, I was just wondering."

"Well, ever since I was a little girl, I'd loved the name Vada. I'd seen a film when I was about six, it had a girl in it called Vada, and ever since then I wanted to call my child Vada - if I had one of course … and I did!"

"What was the film about?"

"Vada, do you expect me to remember that? I'm an old woman."

"You're not old."

"Thank you." She laughed a Mum-type-laugh, and pulled out her hand and placed it on mine.

"Please, try and remember."

"Well I think it was about how this group of teenagers got into all sorts of trouble, but then one girl, Vada, went missing and they all set out to find her … "

"And did they?"

"What?"

"Find her … ?" I asked, intrigued.

"Yes, yes they did."

"What was it called?"

" 'Sweet, sweet, pink.' "

"You're kidding right?"

"Nope, that was its name." I laughed with Mum for ages … it felt nice to laugh, but for some reason I felt guilty … don't ask why, 'cause I don't even know myself.

"I love you, Mum."

"I love you too, Vada."

When we got home, I walked around the house, inspecting it, to make sure nothing had changed, as it felt like I'd been away for weeks. I went upstairs to my bedroom, the sun shone through the window onto my desk … and my beloved diary … My bed was freshly made, with my pillows fluffed up. On my bedside table sat a vase with a beautiful bunch of fresh flowers. My bedroom felt fresh and nice, it felt like me, and the feeling of being back was the nicest ever, even though I knew the journey wasn't over.

I dumped my stuff on the floor by my bed, walked over to my desk, opened up my diary and began to write …

> Dear Diary,
>
> Well I'm back from the hospital; I've been there for what seems like ages. I've missed everyone and I still miss them, and I can't go back to school yet. But hey, at least I'm at home … yeah?
>
> We've worked out that chemotherapy is the best source of treatment. I'll be starting it next week …

As I finished my sentence, Mum knocked on the door.

"Come in," I called.

"Hi, hi … Vada!" Mum said, glowing with delight to have me back.

"Hi!" I answered.

"Are you alright? Do you want me to get you something?"

"No, I'm fine … ," I said, wanting to be left alone so I could carry on writing my diary.

"A drink … A sandwich?" she nagged.

"No, I'm fine!" I said, getting more and more annoyed.

"Sure?"

"Yes, I am not an invalid, you know! I can do things for myself!" I shouted.

"OK, I'm sorry."

"Mum, I am fine, I have just come home, and want to be left alone for a bit, if you want to do anything, you can just do that."

"Fair enough. But hey, if you do need anything, just give me a shout." I smiled and looked at her, with a 'go-away-leave-me-alone' look. And at that, she left. Maybe I was too harsh on her … I just needed to be alone. I carried on writing my diary.

> Now, where was I? That's right, I was just saying about my treatment, I am pretty scared really. I mean … What if it doesn't work? I want to get better, I may as well try this, what's the harm?
>
> Vada

I closed my diary, and then I looked into my mirror sitting on my desk collecting dust. I blew the dust off, picked it up, and looked deep into it … in a world of my own. I grabbed a piece of my hair, and repeated to myself. "What is the harm? What *is* the harm?! What is the **bloody** harm!!" Man, the truth really hurt. But the weirdest thing was that I wasn't quite sure of what the truth really was! I tried to refuse my tears, but they still came, pouring down my face, hitting my desk. I closed my eyes, as several more fell … why in the world has this happened to me? … Why me? … Why me?

I leaned over to my CD collection, fingered through each CD, and took one out; I picked 'I don't want to miss a thing' by Aerosmith. I loved that song, so sad but so beautiful. I closed my eyes, and sat at my desk, listening to my music, piercing my ears. I hated the silence, and I hated the sound—but loved the music. Tears floated down my cheeks, battling to get to the bottom first. I was thinking of nothing and everything, all at the same time. If that was possible.

For the rest of the afternoon and evening I pottered about in my room, saw a little TV and went to bed at about 9:00, because it always took me several hours to get to sleep. I was tossing and turning all night ... Worrying about the months ahead of me. I was worrying about 'What's harm ? What's the harm?' and who knows what the harm ever is?

The next day I slept until about 10:30. It was lovely to be back home, in my silent and private room. I could actually sleep a *little* better than in the hospital ... Thank God.

That afternoon I had a surprise, a nice surprise though. My grandparents came to visit, my Mum's Mum and Dad. I hadn't seen them for what seemed ages, so it was really nice to see them.

"We have missed you so much, being far away and worrying all the time about our little granddaughter, and when we heard that you had been moved to the hospital, we were desperate to come down and see you, but we were very tied up. But we have been praying and thinking about you often my dear, often," Grandma said, hugging me tightly.

"I have missed you too," I said. "But I'm OK, Grandma, honestly."

We had tea and talked for ages and ages, though they did most of the talking, telling us about my little new cousin and other relatives, but that was normal for my grandparents; it was better than talking about me anyway.

Then at about 7:00pm, Sam came over. It was nice to see him, as it seemed like ages since I had last seen him. We sat and talked for a while.

"I've missed you."

"Me too," I replied.

"When is your first appointment?"

"Next Monday."

"Soon then?"

"Yep."

"Will you be coming back to school?"

"Not yet, as the treatment makes me feel pretty unwell."

"Oh, come here." I got out of my seat and sat on his lap, as he directed. We kissed.

"I'm so glad I have you."

"Me too." I smiled.

We talked up in my room for about an hour.

Sam was a little like a brother to me. I could talk to him about anything, and vice versa. He'd give me great advice and would never interrupt; he'd just let me talk. I probably dominated the conversation a little too much, but he didn't seem to mind. I could always be myself around Sam, which was so great!

The day seemed to rush past very quickly, which in a way was good, but in another way not so good, as I dreaded next Monday!

What if my hair does fall out ... I'd be so embarrassed around Sam and my other friends and family. They'd probably be embarrassed about me too, going round with a pale, thin body! This image in my head was torturing me ... Why can't I stay how I look, and get better, why does everything else have to change too?! But I suppose I have to try and be positive, I have to try and think positive, and keep my hood up!

Wednesday was pretty boring really. I had nothing to do all day. Grandma and Granddad had left that morning, Mum and Dad were working, and Nick was at school, then at his girlfriend's house. I saw TV all day and wrote a little in my diary. Boring, or what! You may think it's heaven but, believe me the thought of doing that for the next six months made me want to vomit itself. The only thing that I wanted to do was sleep, get better, and go back to school.

A few more days passed, nothing really happened, so not much to report or write about. In two days I was due back at the hospital for my first treatment! Jonna was coming over for the afternoon. She and I were gonna have a good catch up and be proper girls for the afternoon, and as it was Saturday, she could stay over a little later.

Unfortunately though, Mum wouldn't let her stay the night, as she reckoned I needed to go to bed early, so that I wouldn't get too tired … Which really sucks … Because I just want to have some fun.

Jonna came over at 2 o'clock, we saw a couple of films, you know, the classics, *Titanic* with Kate Winslet and Leonardo Dicaprio, and *Sleepless in Seattle* with Meg Ryan and Tom Hanks! *Sleepless in Seattle* is my favourite film ever! It's so lovely. It is about a man (Tom Hanks) who has just lost his wife, and his son calls up this radio station, and wishes that his Dad would get a new wife, and be happy again. Millions of women rang and wrote to him but there was one that stuck out (Meg Ryan). Eventually they meet at the top of the Empire State Building! Oh, how romantic!

We painted our nails and toenails and then did a face mask each! It felt so great to beautify myself up before Monday! I felt like me again, I felt like I should feel. I felt like a teenage girl with no problems, but actually inside of me I was screaming and gasping for air. It was like a part of me had been ripped away and now I'd found it again. I can't believe that when I found out about my cancer, that I thought it would just go away. It won't. But hey, at least I'm doing something about it now. Let's just hope it works!

On Sunday I did something that I hadn't done for what seemed a very long time ... I went to church. I hadn't been for more than a month. I longed to see my friends but most of all to talk to God. I know I don't need to go to church to do that but it felt nice doing it there ... I woke up at 9 and got ready to go, as it started at 10. My joints were aching, and I had an awful cough. My cough started a few weeks ago but it wasn't this bad ... I was coughing through the whole service... How embarrassing! But then ... something shocked me, a nice shock though. Everyone was sitting or kneeling to pray, when my name came up in the prayer by my vicar. I was so stunned that he was doing that ... in a way I was pleased that he was praying for me, but he was doing it out loud ... to the whole congregation ... which felt a bit weird ... But special!

After the service, my friends and I hung about laughing, and talking ... I felt very tired and weak though, but I was OK ... It will really hit me when I have my treatment, which is when it'll really hurt!

A little later the vicar came to say hello to me. He seemed really nice. I didn't know him too well. He said that he was praying for me. I know it's nice, but I felt a bit scared that this man was praying for me, and I didn't really know who he was, but hey, I suppose that's OK.

When I got home I noticed my name was in the 'Please Pray For' section in the service sheet. Let's hope all these people's prayers helped. Sometimes I'd get scared about what I believed. What if it was all not true...? You know? No God, no Jesus, no Bible and no Heaven. Think of all those people and me, in pain that their belief had been smothered! I suppose it is all a case of believing – but I can't help having a little doubt sometimes ... but I wish I didn't ... have doubt, I mean. God has changed me, and as long as I believe, I will always be ME and will be happy.

Chapter Four

Selfish little rag dolls

MY ALARM CLOCK RANG, SHARP INTO MY EAR ... I reached out my hand, and whacked the button with my finger. The piercing sound stopped, leaving an awkward silence, as I realised what I had woken up to.

Monday! And you know what that meant? First day of my treatment! I got out of my bed, and went into my parents' room where my Mum was in bed reading. I sat down on the edge of her bed and said, "Morning."

"Not a good morning?" she asked.

"It depends ..."

"It'll all go fine, Vada ... OK?"

"I am hoping so." I squeezed her hand and left the room.

I went downstairs to watch some telly. I was just sitting there, watching something pointless on telly, when for some absurd reason I started to cry, a lot! I couldn't stop, it was nearly like I was howling. Mum came running down the stairs to me. She placed her hands around the back of my head and we sat there, rocking. I hugged her... for several minutes we just sat there, nothing was said, that's what I loved so much about my Mum, she'd always know what was wrong, and nothing had to be said to understand it either. She wouldn't ask me questions, she would just be there, a loving and caring mother. It's great.

"Come on Vada, come and get ready." Mum helped me up to my room. I got dressed, but all I could think about was me without hair: I imagined brushing my 'hair' – but then there would be nothing to brush ... I would just be scraping my bare scalp. I got so scared that I dropped my brush and jumper, and crawled into my bed. Just before 11:00, which was when we were meant to leave as the appointment was at 11:30, Mum came into my room and found me still sitting huddled up in bed.

"Vada! What in the world are you doing? We have to leave NOW!" she said picking up my jumper lying all creased up on the floor.

"I don't want to go." I felt like a little girl on her first day of school.

"You know that you have to ... to get better, I mean."

"I know ... but I'm scared, Mum," I whispered.

"Vada, think about it ... You have to do this to get better. You have to try and fight it; don't let the cancer win."

I paused before I said anything, and thought about what she'd just said to me. I'd never thought about the cancer that way, I'd always thought negatively. But it was true. The worst thing here would be to let the cancer win this fight. My life suddenly came into perspective: I had to fight it, and be strong. I smiled at Mum, as I wiped a tear off my face. I got up out of bed, put my clothes on, and headed for the car.

As we were driving to the hospital, Mum suddenly asked, keeping an eye on the road, "So what changed your mind to come?"

"Everything," I answered boldly.

We both laughed, and smiled.

"I'm proud of you Vada, you know that, don't you?"

"Thank you."

When we arrived at the hospital, we were unsure where to go, so we went to the main desk.

"How may I help?" the smiling lady said, at last, as we'd had to queue.

Mum handed her a piece of paper, with info about my treatment and me.

"The Chemotherapy Department is in Building 3, first floor. Ask at the desk."

She couldn't have said it louder, for crying out loud. I mean, hello, delicate subject here. I'd rather that the whole waiting room didn't know!

"Thank you," Mum said, seeming a little shocked too. I grabbed Mum's hand as we walked to the 'Chemo Department'.

That's just scary, I mean there will be loads of cancer patients in there, just like me, maybe even some my age. We arrived outside the building, with a small sign by the side of the door, saying 'Chemotherapy – Dr Miles'. We walked through the automatic doors, and were greeted by posters with information on different cancers and different treatments. I ignored them, as I didn't need to look at them, and other patients' problems. I had enough of my own. We walked down a long corridor, until Dr Miles' door jumped out at us. Mum knocked at it carefully.

"Come in," we heard a small voice say.

Mum went in first, and I followed.

"Ahh Vada, I've been expecting you. Sit down, sit down."

"Thank you," Mum said, kindly.

"So, how are we doing?" she asked, looking at my file.

It was a bit like going to the doctor with a cough, you'd sit down in a chair by the doctor's desk, you'd talk to the doctor, and then she or he would do their stuff. But in this case the 'stuff' was a little more painful than normal.

"Vada is doing well, she's been very nervous about coming here, but we're here."

"Mum!" I said, looking at her a little annoyed that she'd said that.

"That's understandable, everyone's nervous at first," she reassured me. I smiled.

"So, how have you been feeling? Any chest pains or coughs?"

"I've had quite a bad cough over the last few weeks. And I sometimes find it hard to breathe, but I don't get chest pains too often," I managed to say.

"Anything else?"

"I've been tired, and I sometimes wake up in the night sweaty and hot."

"Any fever?" she asked.

Mum answered, looking over at me as she said it. "No, not really."

"OK, good, shall we get on?"

"Will I live …?" I asked, in a hurry.

"Vada, you have something called Hodgkin's Disease. It's a type of lymphoma cancer, and 78% of patients live. So please try not to worry."

I realised that she hadn't actually answered my question, she had twisted it. I hated it how doctors did that.

"Have a seat here, Vada."

I got out of my chair, shaking a little, and slowly lowered myself onto the doctor's bed. Dr Miles pulled a small trolley out from under the bed. It had a white cloth covering it. She removed the cloth. On the trolley lay several syringes, needles, and tablets, all organised into different piles, all set up and how it seemed to me, ready to be fired into another person. I felt like something unimportant and useless. I felt like a rag-doll being prodded and pricked.

"Nearly done," she said. I felt Mum's hand squeeze mine. I was too much 'somewhere else' to squeeze hers back. The world seemed fuzzy and faded, I had my eyes closed a little, and I was half-sitting and half-lying. I heard a few noises around me, but felt so weak and tired that I made no effort to even remotely *try* and make out what they were. When Dr Miles had finished injecting me, and taking blood samples with needles, I lay for a few minutes and then slowly sat up and looked around the room. My arms were aching, and my chest felt like someone had thumped me really hard.

"How are you feeling?" she asked kindly, but fakely.

"Awful," I said.

"It will feel much better next time, it's because it's your first that you feel like this."

What does she know, I thought to myself. Had she ever been on this side of the needle?

She handed me a glass of water, and opened up her other hand. Inside her palm lay around ten tablets, some small, some large, some green, some white. I threw up there and then, over my lap and glass of water.

"It's OK, it's OK," Mum said, rubbing me on the back.

"I'll just get a cloth." Dr Miles stood up and walked over to the sink, placing the ten tablets to one side. She picked up a cloth, wet it under the tap, and came back to us. She dabbed the cloth over my lap, removing some of the 'sick'. She and Mum cleared the rest up as I sat on the bed, all pale.

"Would you like to try again?"

I nodded, as I wanted to get it over and done with and go home to bed. I chose a tablet, placed it inside my mouth, and had a small sip of water. The tablet slid down easily. But I felt sick at the thought of swallowing nine more. I swallowed each tablet, one by one, sipping water and breathing deeply in between each gulp.

"All done," Dr Miles said.

I smiled, and then said, feeling a little better now, "I'm sorry for being sick".

"Vada, don't worry, it's understandable, don't worry, it's fine, nothing to lose sleep over." I'll be losing enough sleep anyway, so I left it.

With Mum's help, I stood up and walked towards the door.

"So I'll see you in a month's time then, but till then you must take it easy and have lots of sleep … OK?"

"Yeah," I said.

"Thank you," Mum said.

"Just ring in to the office, and they'll book you an appointment."

"Thank you," Mum said again.

Mum held my arms as I struggled to walk, tired and weak. I'd had blood removed, which was probably why I was feeling like that. We walked down the corridor. As we got to the waiting room, we heard a call from Dr Miles' office. It wasn't to us, as I saw another girl around my age, maybe a little older, get out of her seat in the waiting room, and head towards the treatment room. We looked at each other, as she brushed past me. I heard her father say to her, "Come on, Sara".

Her name was Sara, I'd always loved that name. It wasn't *Sarah*, it was *Sara*. I loved how it sounded. I wanted to stop Sara, to introduce myself, but her father seemed pretty scary, plus I felt awful. Maybe I'd ask Marie whether she knew someone called Sara. You never know, do you?

As Mum and I headed home, I didn't know what to say, 1) because I felt so unwell, but 2) because I felt embarrassed as I'd thrown up all over myself. But at last Mum said something.

"How are you feeling?"

"Sick."

"We are soon home, and you can go straight to bed, and sleep."

I thought about it, and looked at the clock on the car dashboard. It was 12:32pm. Oh my gosh, that session had taken nearly an hour! No wonder I was tired.

When we got home, I went to the kitchen for a drink, and then I went up to my bedroom. Mum followed.

"Would you like to stay up here, or would you rather that we moved you onto the sofa downstairs?"

"The sofa, I don't want to sleep."

Mum grabbed my duvet and pillow, as I changed into my nightie.

I felt more weak than physically sick. But maybe that would all change? I didn't want to eat anything, I wasn't hungry at all. Plus I was too scared that I'd throw it all up. I saw TV and videos for the rest of the afternoon and evening. Very, very boring, but it was all that I felt capable of doing, in the state I was in.

The next day, I felt even worse. I was throwing up often and had a high fever all day. I didn't do anything, I just lay in bed or on the sofa listening to my CDs, as I didn't even have enough energy to keep my eyes open to stare at the TV. I just let the music play, and work itself into my head. As I listened to the songs, I thought about stuff. It was great to have time to think. But I just wish that I'd felt a bit better, so I could *do* something about my thoughts. If that makes any sense at all.

❁   ❁   ❁

Several days passed as I just lay in bed or on the sofa, watching TV or listening to my music. By the following Monday I felt a lot better, other than being extremely tired all of the time. The nausea and loss of appetite, had nearly all gone. I was eating a little more each day, as Mum said that if I didn't eat at all, I'd become weaker and worse. In the evening, several people phoned for me. Jonna called, to see how I was. She asked whether she could come and visit me, but I said that she should wait a little, as I was still very tired. Then Sam phoned. He'd phoned last week, several times, but I wasn't up to talking much, so Mum told him to ring later in the week, instead. He also asked whether he could come and visit. However much I longed to see him, I decided it would be wrong to say yes to him, and not to Jonna. So I decided to say no, but that I'd call him when I could see him.

Then Marie phoned.

"Vada, is that you? How are you? Are you well? How was your first treatment? Hmm?" She seemed so enthusiastic. It was like she was scared of silence!

"It went well, I'm doing well," I answered, trying to cover most of the questions asked.

"Good, good! So do you want to go swimming this Wednesday?"

"Yeah, OK, but I'm feeling very tired."

"I know. I won't overwork you, we'll only do as much as you feel up to, OK?"

"OK … Marie? Do you know somebody, around my age, called Sara?"

"Sara? Oh yes, Sara Menor. She's a patient who I swim with. How do you know her?"

"Oh, I don't. I just saw her at the hospital and, well, I was intrigued. Is there any way … actually, don't worry!"

"Oh, go on, tell me."

"No, honestly, it doesn't matter."

"OK, well, I will pick you up at about 10:30, OK?"

"Yep."

"See you then, then."

"See ya."

I was going to ask whether I could meet Sara, but I sort of changed my mind. That could just be odd. Plus, I didn't even know her, and she'd probably just think I was a total freak for getting in contact with her. Oh well, maybe we'd meet by chance, one day.

Later that evening I looked 'chemotherapy' up in the dictionary. It said: 'Chemotherapy – treatment of a disease by chemical means'.

What did that mean? It said nothing about cancer, nothing about getting better. Oh well, it's a dictionary. What does it know?! (A lot.) I closed the dictionary, and held it for a moment.

"What does it know?" I repeated to myself. I threw it onto the floor, which it hit with a bang, as Mum came in.

"What are you doing, Vada?"

"Nothing … sorry Mum." I wasn't crying, I was doing everything *but* crying. I was just angry! I was angry that I had cancer and, for some reason, I blamed it on the dictionary.

I woke up several times that night. Sweating and hot, I also had bad loss of breath. I had a paper bag next to my bed which, whenever I'd lose my breath or have difficulty breathing, I'd pick up, place around my mouth and breath into slowly, catching my breath again. And, surprisingly, it actually worked. After a few nights like that, I'd got used to it, and now I had the paper bag, I didn't feel the need to wake Mum.

At last Wednesday came. I'd been looking forward to it a lot, as I was longing for a day with a plan. At 10:30, the doorbell went. I opened the door, and there stood Marie. She took my bag out of my hand, and said, "Come on!"

I waved bye to Mum, as I got into the car with Marie.

"See you soon," Mum said back. "Have fun."

"We will," I answered, as the car zoomed off, and Marie waved.

"So, what's your favourite stroke?"

"I love breaststroke."

"Great, that's one of my favourites too."

"Is anyone else going to be there?" I asked.

"No, it's just you and me. There will be other people in the pool, but not people I teach. Is that OK?"

"Fine."

"Good." The pool wasn't far away from my house. About five minutes. It was an average size pool. There were actually two pools – one small, which was called the 'learners pool', and one called the 'main pool'. The main pool was cold, but the learners pool was warm. It was always full of little babies with their mothers. There is a joke that the pool is so warm because all the little children pee in it. I certainly hoped that that joke was not true, as to my surprise, I was swimming in the learners pool.

My swimsuit was a black one, with orange stripes on the side. It was a 'Speedo' swimsuit. Mum had recently bought it for me, as I was going to do swimming weekly.

I swam for about 30 minutes or so. I did lengths, and just mucked about for a little. Marie wouldn't let me go underwater, she said that wouldn't do me any good at all. I wondered why and realised that it was probably because I already had a shortage of breath, and I didn't need to lose any more.

After my swim, Marie bought me a Coke and a Mars bar, and we sat in the café for about half an hour, talking. I told her about Sam and about all my friends at school. Later, I asked her, "You know Sara, well I was wondering whether she was on the basketball team too?"

"Sara ... Sara Menor, you mean?"

"Yep."

"She is, yes ... Would you like to meet her?" she said, reading my mind. Mind you, it was probably a very easy thing to do, as I was always asking after her.

"I'd love to."

"Well, this Friday, every Friday actually, there is a practice, and I'm sure that you'd be very welcome to come along."

"That would be great," I said.

At that, Mum came through the cafeteria doors, and I shortly left with her.

"See ya Friday then, 10:30," Marie shouted out at us.

"Yep, see ya then." For the first time in my life, I realised how important this treatment was. I longed to go for my second treatment, so I could get better. Why it suddenly hit me then, I don't really know. All I know is that I am going to get better whatever it takes, and however long it will take me. I felt like me, I felt like I was in charge of me again, I could make the decisions, and that's what I did from then on!

I was pretty tired after all that swimming. My joints were hurting, and my cough was a bit worse. I saw TV, and read a little. It felt odd to have been out. I'd gone out with Mum or Dad sometimes, but that was only to get the shopping … And even that seemed a bit ambitious as going swimming was quite tough and used up a lot of energy. As I thought about this, I realised that maybe I was getting a little better and a little stronger, I mean I'd have to be, to be able to go swimming. I was improving. Whether it was a lot or a little I don't know yet, but I was improving. That counts for something, doesn't it? I got off the sofa, and ran into the kitchen where Mum was, as she'd got a day off work to pick me up.

"What is it? What is it?" Mum said, as I came running into the room.

"I want to go back to school, Mum, I want to go back, I feel a lot better," which was a tiny bit of a lie, but hey, if you compared it with last week, I was tons better!

"Vada, you are still very unwell, it's going to take more than one treatment to get you fully better. School is out of the question."

"Mum, please, I long to go back to school, to see my friends and to get back into my normal routine again, get my life back on track, it would do me good, Mum."

"Vada, there is no way that you are going back to school, your routine it going to take a long time to be the same again, and even if it did help, you'd become too tired, and sick."

"What do you know, I don't see you having cancer! I want to go back, I'm sick of watching TV constantly, watching both episodes of 'Neighbours' each day, I'm sick of it, I want to live my life how it was."

"Vada, don't speak to me that way. It's not my fault this … so don't get angry at me. I know this is hard for you, I know that you are frustrated at being home all the time, but you're just not well enough to go back to school *yet*."

"It's just so boring."

"Well you're going to be going out swimming and things with Marie. And if you like, then you and I could do things together. I can get a few days off work, and be with you so you don't have to be alone." Mum looked at me, she was trying so hard, I should at least give her credit for that. "We could even get you some school work, which you can do at home so you can catch up a bit, before going back to school. How does that sound, huh?" I thought about it, it sounded OK.

"But Mum, if I'm going to be doing all that, then what will the difference be if I went to school."

"Vada, you don't realise it yet, but the thing is you will become very tired, and going to school will make you more tired. If you stay at home, you'll be able to stop doing stuff when you become tired, and you can rest. Becoming too tired isn't good, as you have to try and keep strong, for your next treatment, I mean. Do you get me Vada?" I looked up, tried hard not to cry, and said:

"Yes, I understand, I just kid myself that there's a way out, and unfortunately there isn't."

"I know Vada, but I promise that from now on, I'll try and make it less boring, and then when you feel up to it, and Dr Miles and Marie think you are strong enough, you can go back to school. OK?"

"OK." This 'making my own decisions' seemed a little harder than I'd thought.

I slept OK that evening, but I kept on wanting to cry for some reason. I suppose I had a reason, but hadn't I cried enough? I mean, is there a limit on how much each person is allowed to cry? I don't really see the point in crying, because all you're doing is crying in pain, and the next day no one is ever gonna know that you cried, unless you tell them. It is a waste of time, though we all still cry. I don't know, whatever it was, I felt better the following morning.

When I went downstairs the table was laid out beautifully, with candles and pretty serviettes. As I stepped into the room I realised what day it was, it was my brother's birthday. I had totally forgotten. The amount of guilt that swept over me at that point was indescribable, I'd been too hung up with my own problems to think about anyone else. I crept into the kitchen quietly, saw my brother buttering some toast, with presents surrounding him. I turned around swiftly and headed back up the stairs, but as I ran, my Mum called after me. I stopped to let her speak.

"Where are you going, Vada?"

"I'm such an awful person, Mum, I forgot his birthday. I've been too hung up with myself to even think about anybody else! I'm such an idiot!"

"Vada, you're not at all an idiot, it's understandable, OK?"

"Stop telling me it's understandable, I'm a bitch, I'm a cow, I'm an idiot, I'm so selfish! I hate myself—I mean, look at me!" I saw Mum look at me slightly, I remembered looking in the mirror that morning, I was pale and thin, my face was all white, and my body was all bony. I hated myself, I was such an idiot.

"You are none of those things, you are you, you are Vada. You are sick, and you are working hard to get better, it's OK."

"But how could I forget Nick's birthday?" I asked

"What day of the week is it, Vada?" Mum asked. What a silly question! But then I realised that I couldn't actually answer it. "Exactly, Vada, it doesn't matter that you don't remember the day, Nick will understand this, OK?" Mum held out her hand towards me. I was standing three steps up the stairs. I grabbed her hand as I walked with her to the kitchen.

"Happy Birthday, Nick."

"Thanks, Vada."

We had a nice breakfast, all four of us, Mum, Dad, Nick and me. Nick didn't ask about why there was no present from me. But deep down, I don't think he needed to.

Later that day, I had an unexpected visit from Sam. He came at about 4:00, just after school. It was so nice to see him as it had been a while.

"How are you, Sam?" I asked. He didn't answer me, instead, he pulled out from behind his back a beautiful single red rose.

"This is for you," he said, "do you like it?" I moved quickly forward and kissed him, he didn't open his eyes, he just stood there. It was so sweet, he was so sweet.

"I gather that's a 'yes' then?"

"It's beautiful Sam, you are so sweet!" He kissed me again … I grabbed his hand, and pulled him up to my room, we sat on my bed, kissing, for about half an hour, with gaps for a couple of words in between. We didn't do anything naughty, Sam wouldn't ever pressure me into sleeping with him, unless I wanted to, which I didn't right now. He wasn't that sort of guy. Plus, we wouldn't want to as we were both underage, we were only 15 years old.

"I have to go … " he said, still kissing me.

"Don't … Stay … I've missed you."

"I have to go, I promised Mum that I'd help with the supper at 5." We stopped kissing, and Sam got up off my bed.

"Will you come and see me again?"

"If you want me to, yes I will."

"When?"

"What are you doing on Saturday?"

"Nothing … "

"Shall I come over then?"

"Sure, what time?"

"Up to you."

"Eleven."

"See you then … yeah?"

"Yeah." We kissed one last time. As he left I said, "Thank you for being such a great boyfriend to me, I don't know what I'd do if I didn't have your support … you believe in me."

"I'll see you Saturday," he said, embarrassed that I had just flattered him quite so much.

"See ya," I whispered, and slumped back onto my bed, smiled and lay there for a few minutes just feeling happy and strong.

The next day, Mum was determined to make me happy, and do something with me, (not that I wasn't happy enough). We went out for lunch, to this little café in the centre of town. We had a good talk, while eating loads. After the meal, Mum took me to a shop she loved.

"Close your eyes," she said. "Closed?"

"Yep," I answered. I stood for a minute or so, while she got the lady at the counter to get something from the back.

"Open," she said. I opened my eyes to see Mum staring at me, smiling … I wasn't quite sure what she'd done. She directed my eyes to my wrist where a silver bracelet was hanging with seven little 'things' attached to it.

"What is it?" I asked.

"Don't you like it?" Mum answered.

"I love it … but I'm just not quite sure what it is," I sniggered.

"It has seven little symbols hanging from it, each one represents something that has been happening or has happened through your life. I have been collecting them for ages and was going to give it to you when you were older, but I decided to give it to you now." I looked down at the bracelet, and studied each symbol closely. Each one was beautifully made, some were just silver or gold, and others had a few colours on them.

"Mum, it's beautiful … they're beautiful."

"I'd hoped you'd like it."

"But it must have taken you ages," I said.

"Well, I put quite a lot of thought into it. But I had to, to make it more special."

"Thank you." I felt a tear coming to my eye, but I didn't want to cry, not now, not in public. But it's impossible to stop tears, so I cried, not too much, just a little. They were happy tears though. We left the shop, and headed for the car. I stopped as I realised what one of the symbols was. It was of a girl with lots of beautiful hair, she was smiling. It was the last symbol on the bracelet. The first one was a little bottle (a baby's bottle), I gather that it represented my birth. The second symbol was of a girl holding hands with another girl, they were both wearing school bags. I realised that it must have represented me at school, with a friend. The third symbol was a small cross. That represented my confirmation and I suppose my faith in God. It could also represent the deaths of many people in my family. The fourth symbol was a small, gold heart. I had no idea what it represented though. Maybe a first boyfriend. The fifth symbol was a girl with a tear running down her face, I gathered for when I found out about my illness. The sixth symbol was a basketball, for the club I will go to, in between treatments.

Finally … The seventh. Simply of a girl smiling.

"They're not in order, they're just things that have happened, or things you like." Mum hesitated.

"It's so nice. Thank you."

"You can carry on adding to them if you like." I smiled, and we held hands as we walked towards the car. We got in and drove to basketball practice.

The silence in the car was nice, it was a warm silence. It was the sort of silence where you didn't need to say anything, to carry across your feelings. I heard from a magazine or something, that the best sort of friend is one that you can spend an hour or so with, and barely say anything. Then you can walk away and feel that you've just had the best conversation ever. I suppose it's true. I let this silence talk for itself.

When I arrived at basketball, I was so nervous, what if I made a total fool out of myself? What if the people there didn't like me? I went into the changing room, got a sports-kit on and went out into the hall. I'd always hated wearing shorts, so I never did, I always wore my *Adidas* tracksuit bottoms and today I wore a pink top with it, to brighten myself up a bit.

I walked out into the large hall and Marie approached me.

"It's so nice to see you Vada. So, you all set?"

"I suppose so."

"Here, come and meet a few of the team." I walked over, nearly feeling that I wanted to hide behind her, but decided to be strong … as I walked, I approached a small crowd of about five girls and three boys. I looked at each one as Marie introduced me.

"This is Vada, she's going to join us for a while." I smiled and she went on, "This is Sally, Erica, Erin, Tom, John, Phil, Alice and Sara." It was Sara, at last I'd been able to meet her. I don't know why I was so eager to meet her in particular, I suppose, something just really struck out about her.

"Hi," Sara said, after all the other lot had gone off.

"Hi," I replied. I couldn't believe that's all I said.

"Marie has told me about you."

"Good stuff, I hope."

"Good stuff."

The conversation was drying up, so I said to her, "I saw you at the hospital before, you have Dr Miles right?"

"Right, oh yeah, I remember." She seemed so nice. "So how many treatments have you had so far?"

"Only one, how about you?"

"I've had five. Its tiring stuff isn't it?"

"Yeah, you're telling me." I looked at her, she was wearing some blue shorts and a grey T-shirt with some sort of logo on it, but I couldn't quite make out what it was. "What does your T-shirt say?" She grabbed each corner, pulled it forwards and read it to me.

"Every third person."

"Why?"

"You really wanna know?"

"Yep."

"Every third person has, or gets, cancer sometime in their life, scary huh?"

"That's so many ... That's awful."

"'Every third person' is a cancer research campaign, my Mum works for it."

"Oh ... Cool ... "

"What's cool?" she asked

"That your Mum works for it."

"Oh, yeah," she laughed.

We played basketball, then got changed and then we got a drink. I was getting a lift home with Marie, so before we left, Marie bought a round of drinks for everyone at the canteen. Erica, Sally and John had already gone home, but Sara, Phil, Tom, Erin and Alice were still there. They all seemed really nice, but it hurt to think that they all had cancer and were ill. What if one of them died? Hang on … I am one of them …

"So, do you wanna meet up sometime? We could … I dunno, you could come over?" Sara said as she stepped into a small, red Renault.

"That'd be great, I'll call you," I replied and Marie and I drove off, waving to Sara. Sara must be about my age, 15, I hadn't actually asked her but I think so. "How old is Sara?" I asked Marie,

"Sara? Um … your age, 15." Marie and I sat in silence for the rest of the journey to my house, which was actually quite surprising, as Marie usually finds it hard to be quiet for more than three minutes!

Chapter Five

Coin slots

NOTHING MUCH HAD BEEN HAPPENING THROUGH THE two weeks between basketball and my second treatment. I'd gone to Sara's house after basketball practice last week, which was totally great. She told me something that I can't seem to get out of my head now. It was: "Don't let the cancer win, as you'll die, not literally, but inside of you, you'll die. A part of you will just give up and die and then you'll feel dead. Just don't let that happen, I did, never again! If you fight it, you'll live forever. Literally? I don't know ... But if you fight it, you'll live on inside, forever!"

It scared me a bit, I mean, what if I wasn't fighting hard enough? What if a part of me did die? But I suppose, because it had stuck with me, it meant something to me. Truth probably, just a scary truth.

I was more scared this time than the first, my hands and legs were trembling a bit. My name was called and I went into Dr Miles' room, thinking to myself that there were only four more treatments after this. Only four more!

The next morning was the worst morning ever. I woke up several times in the night, throwing up and feeling really hot. But at 8:30 I woke up and looked down at my pillow. It was covered in hair, locks of it were just lying there, like dead soldiers! I screamed, as Mum came running in... I was kneeling on my bed just screaming and crying so loud, you could have heard me on the other side of the world. Mum took one look at my pillow and just came to me, she hugged and held me, like I was a baby in her arms again.

"We knew this could happen, Vada. Try and be strong."

"I know, I know." I cried so much, I could hardly get the words out. "I know, I was expecting it, I was prepared, I just forced myself to believe that it wouldn't happen. Then when it does, you feel like you've just been stabbed in the back, really hard, really hard."

"I know Vada, I understand." She rocked me, like I was a baby in her arms.

For the rest of that day, I cried so much my eyes felt like coin-slots. I didn't want anyone to see me like this. I had a little hair left, but not much, I felt so stupid. Mum was great though. I wore a bandanna for the day, even thought it didn't suit me at all. But it was better than looking like an 80-year-old bald man.

Sam called that evening. I didn't tell him about my hair, or should I say, my 'not' hair. I should have told him though, I mean he is my boyfriend … I just, I just, felt really stupid, I mean, do you blame me?

For the next few days, Sara's friendship and mine grew. She came to my house often, and I went to her's. We talked loads.

Today was a Tuesday; she'd invited me over in the afternoon. I put on my bandanna, tying it carefully at the back, put on my favourite clothes and walked to her house. I was surprised with how much I managed to do nowadays. I think that all the sport I was doing was helping to keep me upright. But I got really tired, really easily, which wasn't too great, but at least I had found a friend who was going through the same as me, and really understood me, which is very hard to find. I felt that Sam and I understood each other well too, but just not in the same way, you know?

"Nice to see you, Vada. Come on in," Sara's Mum said kindly.

"Thanks," I answered, and stepped into their house. Sara had the most beautiful house, it was huge. She had a large room and her garden was the size of a football field. I'd love to have a house like her's.

"Hi, how are you?" Sara asked, coming down the stairs as she saw me.

"Hiya, I'm fine, how about you?"

"Umm, I'm not too great, but Dr Miles says that it was expected." Sara had now had seven treatment, and she was still not well. I'm worried she'll never get better.

We walked up to her room, sat down and then just talked for several hours.

"Are you going to go back to school?" I asked.

"No."

"Why not?"

"Dr Miles says that I am too ill, how about you?" 'Dr Miles says … Dr Miles says …' - is it ever anything else?

"Well, I have been working from home, but it's just not the same, is it?"

"I tried that, didn't help though, do you reckon that you will go back though?"

"I hope so," I said.

We talked until about 12:30 at night, but it took me ages to get to sleep. I wasn't asleep until about 2:00am. I couldn't stop thinking about what we'd been talking about. Especially about going back to school. The next day when I got home, I'd ask Mum and Dad whether I could go back to school.

"Did you have a good time at Sara's?"

"Yeah, it was good ... Mum?"

"What?"

"Can I go back to school?"

"Vada, you know this isn't up to me."

"So?" there was a pause.

"We'll see. We can talk to Dr Miles and see what she says."

"OK," I said disappointedly, as I walked up to my room.

Through the weeks before my third treatment, I hadn't done much. I had just been counting the days before my next treatment so we could discuss going back to school with Dr Miles. She was really hard to get a hold of, so you could only see her with a booked appointment. Mum said that there wasn't much point in seeing her beforehand, as it was only a couple of weeks until I saw her for my treatment.

Sara and I had got together loads; we had mostly just sat and talked, for several hours, which had been great. But Sara had been getting worse and worse. She couldn't see me as much as before because she was so weak. One thing I envied about her was that she hadn't lost her hair, even though she'd had more treatments than I had. She had beautiful hair. It was a golden blonde colour, just past her shoulders. It was so beautiful. I try to avoid all mirrors nowadays, I was just too scared to see myself, I missed my hair. I did have a little hair, but only in patches and even then, it was very thin, and hung off looking very dead.

Sam had been away for a week, so I'd only seen him once or twice and when we did, it wasn't for very long. I didn't say anything about my hair, he eventually realised but he was lovely about it. I had been going to basketball every week and swimming twice a week; I was doing great, or at least, that's what Marie said. I was the best at scoring on our basketball team. We had played against Birmingham and Bristol, and we had beaten them both, pretty good huh? I was pretty chuffed as I'd scored most of the baskets. I was sure I was on the mend and today was just to back my thoughts up.

"Vada, come in," Dr Miles said, directing me and Mum to her room. "Have a seat."

"Thank you," Mum said.

"Before we go ahead with your treatment, I have some good news." It was odd, because she hadn't even noticed that I'd lost my hair. We both smiled, as Dr Miles said this, "I have got some results back from your tumour tests, and they show that it is shrinking considerably, you are well on the mend." She smiled as she handed me an X-ray photo thing. "This is your tumour here," she said, pointing to a smallish grey splodge in the middle of my chest in the picture. "This is how your tumour used to be." She said, pointing to a larger grey splodge. I was no doctor, but I could tell myself how it had shrunk. "I'm very pleased with how this is going. Well done!"

"Will I still have to have all six treatments?" I asked hopefully.

"I'm afraid it's too early to say, but I'd expect so as we don't want to risk underdoing it and it would be silly not to really get rid of it. But think, after this treatment, you are half-way through!" I smiled effortlessly as Mum held out her hand, grabbed mine, squeezed it and gave me a wink.

"Shall we start, Vada?"

"Yeah." I got up and headed for the doctor's bed/trolley thing.

"Can you please remove that bandanna." I looked over at Mum, she smiled and I slowly untied it at the back and placed it next to me on the bed. Dr Miles didn't say anything to me about my loss of hair, but she gave me a sympathetic smile instead.

I swallowed a number of pills and felt needles being slowly prodded into me; she took tests and X-rays too. I didn't feel quite so sick this time, I suppose the good news that I was improving strengthened me in some way.

Just before we left Mum asked Dr Miles something that had totally slipped my mind.

"Do you think Vada is well enough to go back to school?"

"I think that it could be good for Vada, yes. But it's totally up to how much she feels capable of." I smiled, and jumped up and down with joy inside of me.

"That's great," Mum said, noticing my excitement.

When I got home, I couldn't stop thinking about going back to school. But hold on, what will people think? Especially as I've lost most of my hair, will they laugh at me? As I thought about it, I decided to ring Sara, I hadn't spoken to her for a couple of days anyway. She'd know what to say and do, I could rely on her. My head was hurting and my stomach aching, but when I closed my eyes the pain drifted. I picked up the receiver and dialled each digit carefully.

"Hello," Sara's Mum answered.

"Hi, can I speak to Sara please?"

There was a long pause, then, "Is that Vada?" Sara's Mum gave a small sniff.

"Yes … Is everything OK?" I asked, knowing that it wasn't, as the tone of her voice was so low and sad.

"I'm afraid it's not OK … " I gulped and found myself having a struggle to breathe.

"Why?" I asked, trying to be strong, but you could tell by my voice that I wasn't.

"Vada ... Sara passed away during the night, she died in her sleep." I had no idea what to say, and felt my eyes filling up like buckets.

"Peacefully?" I asked, struggling to get the words out.

"Peacefully," she answered. "Vada, will you be alright?"

"No ... no, I don't think I will."

"Thank you for calling."

"Bye." I know it seemed rude not to give my sympathies to her, but I couldn't. I just ... couldn't.

I lowered the receiver and placed it on the handset.

I cried and screamed, I screamed really loudly. My head was spinning round and round like a roundabout and my stomach was hurting so much I could barely breathe.

"Vada, what is it?" Mum came running into the room and hugged me.

"It's Sara, she died in the night ... Sara, she died, SHE DIED!"

"Shhhh ... Shhhh ... It's OK ... It's OK."

"No it's not Mum, it's not OK, Sara was Sara ... there was no one like Sara, we understood each other like no one else, and now she's gone ... I don't think I can handle it anymore, why can't I die too." My Mum started to cry, but she refused to let the tears show, she didn't want me to see her like that.

"Don't say that, Vada, how could that help?"

"I would be out of pain, I would be with Sara, I could keep her company."

"Vada, don't say that … please don't."

"I'm sorry … But I just want to be alone right now." Mum nodded as she let go of me. I walked away, upstairs to my room, and I don't think I came back out for the next 36 hours. Mum insisted on talking to me, but I didn't want to, my brother and Dad even tried too, but I still wouldn't … I didn't want to. My meals would be left outside my door and I'd take them in, a little while after they were placed there. I would only eat half of the food, I wasn't ever that hungry. All I did all day was cry, I'd block out the light and would sit on my beanbag in the far corner of my room and cry.

But that afternoon I was looking through my box which I kept special things in. I was flicking through the various amounts of letters when I came across one from Sara, which she'd written after we'd had a talk about feeling lonely. I read it to myself:

> " … Please try and remember that you need the people around you, you need them to keep strong, don't punish them by blocking them out.
>
> As well as you needing them, they need you, please remember this and remember that I

love you and always will ... "

I felt like she was next to me, saying this. It was exactly what I was doing, I was blocking my family out, they hadn't done anything wrong. Again, Sara's words came to me and stuck with me. That evening I emerged from my bedroom, and went to see my Mum. She was sitting on her bed, crying, but when she saw me she smiled and cried happily. I sat with her for several minutes ... nothing was said, but it felt like I'd had the best conversation in all my life.

I had missed basketball and swimming sessions and was feeling quite a bit worse. We went to see Dr Miles the next day, as luckily she had a cancellation. She gave me some sleeping tablets which would help me sleep, I was nearly positive that they wouldn't work. But that night I slept so well an orchestra couldn't have woken me. The next few days were hell, I was so depressed and down that my body was collapsing. Dr Miles came to see me several times to check on me because my Mum was so worried, but there wasn't really much she could do.

The following day was Sara's funeral. I'd been asked whether I'd like to speak, but I had said no. Mum stuffed me with paracetamols and vitamins as we headed off to church. I was wearing a long black skirt, a pink shirt with a black jacket covering it. I was still crying. I don't think I had actually stopped for the past five days.

When the time came, everyone walked around the coffin in an orderly line just like Sara would've done. A large bouquet of red and white flowers lay on top of the coffin lid. I placed my pink rose on the coffin and said, "Thank you Sara … Goodbye." It was all I managed to say, but to be quite honest, it felt just right.

Then the speeches came, several were made, tears were shed and music was played. I had an urge to say something, to get up there and speak, to talk about one of the greatest people I had ever met. I got out of my seat at the end of the song. 'I believe' had been played beautifully on the organ, with the choir singing to it. And the vicar nodded me up to the front.

"Sara and I always loved that song," I began. "We'd sing it when we were alone, whether we were walking down the street or were trying to get to sleep." I was standing by the altar, facing a congregation of about 200 people. "Sara and I just clicked. She'd know what I was thinking before I had even thought it myself. There was no one who could understand the friendship we had. We would often just sit in silence for several minutes but then walk away feeling like we'd just had the best conversation in the whole world. I love her and will never forget her, ever! She made me realise things, which no one else could, even after her death. I found a letter she'd written to me several weeks back. If it wasn't for that letter I don't think I would be standing here today. I might well have just been cooped up in my room with no light and no company. But instead, I am here, saying goodbye to someone that I love so much."

I looked around the church as I heard a man stand up and clap, then some more, then some more, until the whole room was filled with sound … I didn't want applause, I just wanted her to be remembered, but I think they all knew that … I think they were all just saying their good byes too.

That evening I barely cried at all. The pain was still there, but I just felt better, I felt like I'd properly said goodbye, I felt at ease. I slept quite well, especially if you compared it with the last week. The next day I had quite an unexpected phone call from Mrs Landport. She hadn't spoken to me for ages and I hadn't spoken to her for a while too. I told her about Sara, she was really nice about it all.

"So are you at school?" I asked her.

"Yes, I have a free period," she said.

"I'm going to come back to school soon, cool huh?"

"That's great!"

"I know, I can't wait."

"When do you think you'll come?"

"Umm … maybe in a week or so, it's just that I'm pretty tired and I don't want to overdo it by getting myself into too much, you know?"

"You seem very sorted and independent, well done. I'm looking forward to seeing you," she said, in a very teacherly way, but nicely.

"Me too," I said, and at that our phone call ended. It was nice to talk to her. After the phone call, school was on my mind again. I pictured myself as 'normal' again. I missed everyone and the more I thought about it, the more I wanted to go. "Mum?" I shouted, as I jumped effortlessly down the stairs.

"What?"

"When can I go back?"

"To where?" she asked.

"School."

"Umm, I don't know, it depends on how you're feeling."

"I'm feeling great!"

"Oi, young lady! Don't lie! I mean, you've been very unwell just in the last week. Going back now is a little ambitious."

"Well, when then?"

"Next week." I jumped up and hugged Mum so tightly I think I stopped her blood circulation.

"That's great! Oh Mum, I love you!"

"But that doesn't mean you can overdo things now. I want you to rest lots this week and then you can go back with a bit more energy."

"Sure, whatever!" I didn't care what the conditions were just as long as I could go back.

I ran up to my room, took out my diary and started to write:

> Dear Diary,
>
> Guess what? I'M GOING BACK TO SCHOOL! I don't think I have ever been quite so pleased about going to school. It means I'm getting better and it means I'm going to become better. Which is really great.
>
> But Sara died. Which is just really depressing. I don't think my pain is ever going to go away, but ... I suppose she's out of pain and with God, in the sky, probably having the best time of her life. But ... I miss her.
>
> Bye, Vada

I closed my diary and paused, then I slammed it down on the floor, creasing the pages and damaging the spine. I started to cry. My tears fell like raindrops. I felt like a grey cloud in the sky. I wondered what Sara was doing now. I just sat in my chair for several minutes just weeping quietly ... thinking about Sara. It's weird how I can be so happy, but then sad, really quickly. I don't think I like it! Why did she die, even when we prayed so much! Why did God take her away from us? From the people who loved her!

� ☒ ☒

The phone went and I answered it.

"Hello?"

"Hi Vada, its Sam."

"Sam ... where are you? It's 1:30, you should be in school," I said, in a motherly, but caring tone.

"I am."

"What?" I said, a little confused.

"I'm in the boys' toilets, on my mobile. I said to Miss that I needed the toilet but actually I just wanted to talk to you. I can't stop thinking about you ... Maths is the last thing on my mind!"

"You'll be dead if you're caught!"

"I don't care ... talk to me, I want to know how you are. I called last week but your Mum said that you weren't speaking to anyone."

"Yeah, I'm sorry about that," I interrupted him.

"What was wrong?" There was a pause while I tried to work out how to put it.

"Sara, you know her right?"

"Yeah."

"Well, she died ... " I refused to cry. I had to learn to say even just her name without crying.

"I'm so sorry ... Are you OK?"

"Not really, but I'll ... " I was about to say I'll live, but that would just be the wrong phrase to use in this case. I corrected myself, " ... I'll be OK. Guess what!" I said, on a happier note.

"What?"

"I'm coming back to school next week."

"Oh my God, that's great, can I tell people?"

"If you like ... but isn't that just great?"

"Yeah, it's great! I can't wait to be able to see you, every single day!"

"Same."

"Oh crap ... someone's coming. I'd better go ... I'll call you. Love you."

"Love you too, oh and good luck!" And at that, he went. I felt so lucky to have him, nearly too lucky ...

The next day was a Wednesday, I was meant to be going to basketball, but I wasn't sure whether I could handle it without Sara there. But hey, you can't mess with Marie, she'd rung that morning, to say that she was picking me up at 3:00 and then she just went. I don't think Marie likes going deep, but I suppose she can't too much, as she's around people like Sara and me all week. I don't think I could ever do her job. The doorbell went at 3:00, like she'd promised. I grabbed my bag and left.

When I got there, I was quiet and didn't say much to anyone. Erica and Alice were trying hard to make friends with me and include me in their group, but it just wasn't the same. They hadn't been as good friends with Sara as I had, but they knew her. I don't think they quite understood how sad I was. They were trying, and I should've at least given them credit for that, but I still felt alone.

Basketball practice was OK, but only OK. When I got home I didn't do much. I had some supper and watched some TV... very boring. I was longing to go back to school, to be with my friends and stuff, then I realised that I could, in a few days I could. It may not seem that exciting to you, but I have done nothing but sitting around thinking ... I am just longing to wake up to a day with a plan. When I remembered I could go back, I got excited again and decided to ring Jonna, who I hadn't spoken to for so long.

"Hiya, how are you?" she said as I said 'hi'. "I haven't spoken to you in ages!".

"Me, well, I'm not so bad. You?"

"Other than that I miss you, I'm OK ... Can I see you?"

"Umm ... " I paused, I couldn't decide whether to tell her I was coming back to school or whether to leave it as a surprise. I decided to tell her. "Well, you can see me next week, I'm coming back to school."

"That's so cool! So has the cancer g ... " She paused, a very Jonna thing to do.

"My cancer is going, yes," I said, finishing off her sentence for her.

"What day?"

"I don't know yet ... I suppose I'll just have to surprise you."

"Great! I'll see you next week, yeah?"

"Yeah." And the phone call finished. The more I talked to Jonna, the more I missed Sara. It's just that Sara was so much more open, and could say things freely, like me. But Jonna was too scared she'd upset me to say anything, which actually really annoyed me. But I suppose everyone's different. Which I suppose is quite good ... just annoying. But I can't complain, I can't imagine how boring it would be if everyone was the same, oh man! I stopped that thought, and went to bed.

I slept OK, I suppose, not for that long, but I slept without too many bad dreams eating my mind up. The next few days went by slowly, even though I tried to fill them up with exciting things to do... it didn't quite work. I was feeling a bit better than I had a month ago. I was either improving or I had just got used to feeling sick, one of the two (but I'm hoping it was the first one!)

Chapter Six

Back on track

TUESDAY CAME. THE DAY MUM HAD SAID I COULD start school. I woke up at 7:00 sharp, washed the little hair I had left, got dressed and then I packed my bag, had some breakfast, and walked down to school. The fresh air circulated in my lungs as I breathed it in slowly. I hadn't walked this way to school for so long that it felt like a totally new experience, even though I knew it back to front. The wind blew my bandanna up and down as though the wind was playing with it. And the birds whistled as I walked past them. No one was around – well, not many people anyway. But I liked it that way. I could be alone for a few minutes until I entered the havoc of school.

I slowly approached school. Nervously I went through the gates as people looked at me, maybe just in a normal way, or maybe they were staring. I don't know. I was too paranoid to know. People greeted me from either side. The word 'hello!' started to ring in my ears. Lots of them were just speaking to me anonymously. I stopped walking, caught my breath, and told myself that nothing had changed, not even *I* had changed. "Vada," I heard a voice call. I turned around expecting to see Sam, but instead it was Jonna. "I didn't know you were coming today."

"Well, here I am."

"I like your bandanna, it suits you." Is that all she noticed? My bandanna had me in it! She came over and hugged me tight and said, "I have missed you."

"I have missed you too." As I said it, I realised that I had missed her. I just hadn't had time to think about her, and when I did I was just comparing her with Sara. Now Sara had gone, Jonna was Jonna, and there was no one to compare her with.

I looked around the school, picking out the things I liked and ignoring the things I didn't. No wonder I had missed it here. I had not been here for about three and a half months. "Do you know where Sam is?" I asked eagerly.

"He's in the class room."

"Do you mind if I go and see him?"

"Sure." We walked together to my form room. The fear that swept upon me as I walked down that corridor was indescribable. I pushed the door and entered. I dragged my eyes quickly around the room and saw Sam flicking through a magazine. He wasn't reading it at all, just pretending to, like you do, you know … when you don't want to be talked to. He looked upset. I knew I'd surprise him, maybe cheer him up, if I went over.

"Sam," I said, waving my hand in front of his face.

"Vada … Hi! Umm … you're here."

" I know, … isn't it great?"

"Yeah," he said, effortlessly.

"You could seem a little more pleased," I said cheerfully, trying to make him smile. "Sorry, it's great … It really is." I whispered to Jonna to give Sam and me a minute. She went and talked with Marjorie and a couple of other friends. I sat down next to Sam, put my hand on his knee, and looking into his eyes, said, "What's wrong?"

"I need to talk to you." He got up and grabbed my hand. I followed as we walked outside, and leaned against the bicycle railings in the courtyard. He looked at me deeply. People were running about and shouting around us. But we were together. The sound was just a muffle, which we peacefully ignored.

"Well," I said, prompting him to tell me what was wrong.

"I'm scared, Vada."

"Of what?" There was a long pause as he thought about what to say. "Go on," I said, prompting him again.

"I'm scared that I'll lose you, and I've been scared to tell you that in case I'd upset you. And I didn't want to upset you. I love you, I really do, I love you." He spoke in a rushed 'trying to get it over and done with' tone. "I've thought about you so much. I've even found it hard to concentrate in lessons. I've missed you. Without you here."

"I'm here now," I interrupted.

"Let me finish."

"Sorry," I said.

"I've been bottled up. I haven't had people to talk to. I feel like I am about to pop and overflow if I don't let this all out."

"Then let it all out. I am listening."

"There's not so much to tell, just that I've found it hard. I think you are so strong and brave compared to me, who is just weak and stupid."

"You're not stupid, not at all."

"Well, I feel stupid," he said.

"Don't."

He smiled and went on. "I feel a bit like I've been in your shoes, going through it all with you."

"Maybe that's because you have been going through it all with me. You've never left me, Sam."

"But I feel like a failure."

"Just by you telling me all this shows that you are not a failure. You are the opposite. Without you, I'd be lost. I would probably not be here, as I'd have just let myself give up. Do you get me?" He smiled and put his arms around me.

"I'm glad you're back, don't leave me," he said.

"Same to you," I said. I felt his salty tear touch my lip, as he kissed me.

I don't think I ever realised how sweet and sensitive Sam actually is. He is so truthful and caring. I now realise that I had actually put him in quite a hard situation. I mean I had just talked about me nearly all the time. He would sit and listen, soaking it in like a wet cloth. He must have found it pretty hard. But I hadn't let myself think about that, I'd been too busy with myself. If anybody was the failure, it was me and me only. I'd been selfish. But I felt like our talk had helped even though I'd thought there was no problem before. I felt different inside. I felt like Sam had just ... had just come again and refreshed and strengthened me.

The lessons were pretty boring but I didn't care. I was back in school where every teenager should be when they are 15. I had history after lunch, which excited me in some way, as I could see Mrs Landport. She'd always been like an extra mother to me, but also a brilliant teacher and friend. People greeted me all day long, even people I'd never liked, or who had never liked me. But they were still nice to me. It annoyed me in a way as I got the distinct impression they were only being nice to me because I was ill and could die. I felt isolated with that feeling. As I saw Mrs Landport she came over and shook my hand and hugged me.

"It's so nice to have you back, Vada," she said in a kind teacher voice.

"It's nice to be back," I said.

As I sat down and the class got to work, I looked at my bracelet dangling off my wrist. There was a symbol missing. It was the one of me coming back to school. I remembered what Mum had told me, "You can add more symbols if you like." I picked up a paperclip on the table and fastened it to my bracelet. I thought that went well. Odd, but it was my step forward.

That afternoon we had assembly. I went in silently and sat down. I nearly dozed off in Mr Smith's talks, they are so boring. Mr Smith is our headmaster. He is the most boring teacher I think I have ever met in all of my life. He just blabs on even if people don't listen. He doesn't seem to care at all though.

Then in the middle of a sentence I heard my name. I looked up, stopped fiddling with my ring, and listened carefully.

"Vada has joined us again after being quite unwell. And just to welcome her back, we would like to give her something. Vada, if you would like to come up." People stared at me as I got up and untangled myself through the mess of bags and chairs lined up all messy on the ground. I walked forward to the front. Two girls in the year below me came from the side of the hall and handed me a bouquet of flowers and a large card. I was speechless. I didn't say a thing, other than, "Thank you".

The card was full of signatures, from each person in my year and all the teachers. I was gobsmacked, if also a little annoyed that everybody knew about my illness. But I have to admit that I was touched.

When I got home that evening I didn't do much other than stare at my card, reading each small message carefully. Many were from people who didn't like me, or so I thought. I wasn't quite sure why they signed it if they didn't like me. But I suppose they were just being friendly, it just seemed a bit odd ... you know.

I was so glad to be back at school. It was so nice to have my 'normal' routine back on track ... and knowing that I had to wake up for school in the morning. Before, I would just wake up and spend the day feeling sorry for myself. And I can't say that helped me to get better. Being back at school was a positive feeling which made me think very much ahead.

School went by as usual. I spent a lot of my time doing homework, writing e-mails, and talking on the phone, mostly to Sam, but also a bit to Jonna. Our friendship grew. We became more relaxed around each other, and she could speak more openly about things on her mind. I don't know what changed, but I didn't care. It was just nice to have each other.

Each Saturday I would go to basketball practice, and swimming after school on Friday. I thought how sad it was going to be to have to stop basketball club and swimming. Marie and I get on well, not just as my instructor, but also as a good friend. Even though she doesn't like going deep, she's lovely. But for the first time on Saturday I saw Marie at the side of the court looking pretty down. In the break I went over and talked with her.

"Are you OK?" I asked.

"Me? I'm OK ... I'm OK," she lied.

"Sure?".

There was a pause as she asked me, "Do you miss Sara?"

"Yes, yes I do, very much ... Do you?"

"Yes, I do." I realised what was on her mind ... Sara. I had never thought about how it must be for her when one of us dies. She must feel pretty sad and let down. She works so hard to keep us well, and then when one of us dies she must feel pretty bad.

Marie went on as though she was reading my mind.

"I worked so hard with Sara. I was so positive and sure she would make it. And then she doesn't. Maybe I worked her too hard. Do you think?"

"No, I don't think you did. Without you she probably wouldn't even have made it through a couple of treatments. You are our inspiration to get better, Marie. And without you I don't know where we would be."

"You're right ... I don't know about the inspiration bit, but hey I suppose my job is to help."

"Exactly," I said. She smiled and I got up.

"Do you reckon she is happy where she is?" Marie asked me.

"I reckon she is having the time of her life ... Don't you?"

"Yes, I suppose I do."

Chapter Seven

A little different but the same

THREE MONTHS PASSED. THEY WENT BY QUITE QUICKLY really, now that I was back at school. I worked hard at school, even though I found it quite hard to concentrate sometimes. I worked as hard as I could. I carried on going to basketball and swimming, but each week I did a little less. Marie said that I could carry on being in the basketball team if I liked. But I wasn't sure if I wanted to. Would it not seem a little odd to be constantly around people who had cancer, when I didn't? I thought the more I was away from that maybe the better. But I had this feeling inside of me that I wanted to help people who go through what I was going through … I wanted to help them in some way. But I didn't know how.

The next day was to be my sixth treatment, and hopefully my last one. But I was trying not to keep my hopes too high. I was so close to the end, so close … just hoping that all would be well after tomorrow. That evening I sat and saw some telly. It was a Thursday, and because I was not going to school the next day, I didn't need to do my homework, which was cool. I talked to Sam and Jonna on the phone … but I wasn't in a very sociable mood. So I didn't talk for very long. I slept OK that night even though it took me quite a while to get to sleep.

I woke up at about 9:30.

On good days I wake up and look at myself in the mirror, and see a face, a blank face. But my big hazel eyes stand out, my small simple lips, and my 'normal' nose. But on bad days I wake up, look in the mirror, quickly turning my face away, avoiding the so-called 'disgusting' reflection. My eyes look horrible, they are all cried out, bloodshot and red. And my nose looks really big, and my lips … my lips look horribly un-kissable. I only notice what I want to notice and everything else looks how I 'want' it to look. Other days I wake up and think how what I have been going through has helped me to be stronger. But on other days I wake up and hit my mirror, remembering all I had gone through, all I'd experienced and all I'd hated.

I am getting better, because I am having more good days than bad, but memories never disappear, everything I have gone through will stick with me forever … even if I get better.

My treatment was at 11:30, so I had quite a while.

"Morning," Mum said as she came in and opened my curtains. The sun was shining. "Morning," I groaned.

"Sleep well?" Mum asked as she came over and brushed her hand against my cheek. "OK I suppose … You?"

"Fine. We'll leave at 11:00. OK?"

"OK." I was pleased that it would soon be over, but also scared … What if I went there and I still wasn't well? What if I had to have more treatments? What if my tumour was growing again? I don't think I could handle that, but I suppose whatever happens I shouldn't give up, as I am so close to the end.

When we got there we had to wait for several minutes, which just made the whole scaredness thing a little scarier.

"Sorry that you've had to wait," Dr Miles said, walking with us to her room.

"Don't worry," Mum said, holding my hand. We sat down around her desk as usual and she started to speak.

"How are you feeling today then?"

"OK."

"Good." There was a pause as Dr Miles flicked through some files to find mine. "I'm afraid there's been some bad news."

"Am I OK?" I asked, worried. I looked around the room noticing for the first time how small it actually was. I felt claustrophobic and small, and I wanted to get out.

"Can I have some water?" I asked, interrupting her first words.

"Yes, of course." She got up and went to the corner of the room where she poured me a cup of water from one of those machines they have in places like that. "Here," she said, handing the cup to me.

"Go on," Mum prompted her. I could tell by Mum's face that she was nervous, more nervous than I was by the looks of it.

"Yes, I have been watching Vada's tumour closely, and I am afraid, we have found that your tumour is growing again."

"What does that mean?" Mum asked.

"It means that this won't be your last treatment."

"Are you saying I won't get better," I asked. "Are you saying I'll never recover?"

"I'm not saying that at all ... I'm positive that we can get you better. It's just going to take a little longer than we had originally planned."

"How much longer?" Mum asked.

"Another two treatments or so." Her voice seemed shaky, as though she felt guilty and was scared to tell the truth. "I'm very sorry. I bet you came today overjoyed that it was going to be your last treatment. I'm sorry I ruined that."

"It's not your fault. I'll be fine. I'm just a little disappointed - not in you, more in myself - that's all." I looked down at the floor picking out the colourful patterns on the carpet.

"Don't blame yourself. You can't control how much it grows. We can only try to control it, and I am positive that in the next two months you will be better."

"I hope so," I said, and we went on with the treatment. I couldn't believe I was going to have to come two more times. I was so annoyed … With no one but myself. I barely felt sick at all after this treatment. I had a headache, and my tummy hurt a bit, but I was OK. I felt better than I thought I would after that news, but worse than I thought I would before I heard that news, thinking that this would have been my last one.

I didn't want to go to school on Monday. I lied to Mum that I felt sick, but she could see through me. She was my Mum, she knew me so well … I couldn't fool her. I just did not want people to know I wasn't better. I was sick of all the sympathy people gave, sick of people who hated me … Pretending to care. I just hated it … I just didn't want to go back. Maybe the people had nothing to do with it, maybe I was just on a low. But it certainly felt like they did. I spent bits of the weekend writing music and songs. But most of the time I spent just sitting alone watching TV and depressing myself even more. I had a tendency to play depressing music, to purposely depress me even more. My life just felt like a never-ending journey. I was getting tired, I needed to stop and rest, I needed a break. But I couldn't. .

"So, when you put a spatula of sugar into this beaker of water, what do you think will happen? Vada, would you like to answer that for us?" Mrs. Granes' chirpy voice was just a muffle as I sat slouched over the small table, which I shared with several others. I just grunted. "Vada, what will happen?" Her chirpy voice was a little less chirpy this time.

"Dunno," I answered unhelpfully.

"Vada, can you sit up and listen!" I sat up and closed my eyes, blocking out all sound and light from my mind. I was slipping at school more than I was slipping in myself … If I would just make more of an effort, then maybe I could get better quicker. But I just couldn't, I couldn't be bothered, I'd given up … I'd stupidly given up!

"Vada, what is wrong with you?" Sam asked, waving and clicking his fingers in front of my face, as I sat staring at nothing in the courtyard.

"There's nothing wrong with me, just shut up!"

"Don't give me that crap. There obviously is. I feel as if I have been left in the lurch. Just tell me."

"Look, I'm not better. In fact I am worse. I have to have two more treatments." There was a pause as he grabbed my hand and pulled me up, kissing me hard. I could hear a couple of people cheering in the background, taking the mick as I kissed him back.

"Why didn't you tell me ... can't you trust me anymore?"

"I do trust you; I just can't handle this anymore. I just want to give up," I explained.

"You can't give up."

"Too late, I already have." I could tell I had said the wrong thing. I could tell that I'd hurt him. "I'm sorry, you know I don't want to give up, it's just hard."

"I can't lose you Vada. You've made me understand so much about myself ... That I never knew."

"No, you've found it out. I have just been there," I said.

"Please can't you understand this, can't you please just try?" His voice was a little shaky.

"I'll try," I said. Whether I would actually try was another matter. We will just have to see.

For the rest of the week I ate very little, making myself low on purpose. I didn't really speak to anyone but Sam. Sam was great, even though I wasn't trying. He didn't like that, but he still stuck by me. So did everyone else, just Sam was different, you know. But then on Monday I felt different. I can't explain. It was indescribable how I felt. Something inside was different. It was a bit like the devil had been kicked out and an angel had been let in. It was odd, but nice. I felt happy, or at least happier. I felt better. But it was impossible, I couldn't have been better, my tumour was growing, for crying out loud, not shrinking. It was impossible that I was better. It was impossible. Yet I felt different. I felt just right again.

I went to school, and laughed and talked as I always had before I became ill. I listened in lessons and I spoke to people at break. It was as though I was back to my old self, as if I was Vada again. On Wednesday I went to Jonna's house. Marjorie, Claire, Sam, Tom and Emily all came too. Tom and Claire are going out. Emily fancies Tom, but Claire doesn't know. It's a very complicated situation. But it felt nice to be back in it all. We saw a movie and talked, just mucking about really. Sam had never really been a part of our group, but it felt right to invite him along that night, and it actually went very well. I could totally relax and be myself around them all. Sam was the only one who really knew what was going on with me. Jonna knew a bit but not as much as Sam. I told Sam I felt better and he seemed really pleased and happy. I suppose it was better than me being in a low and starving myself. Still, he did seem very much happier.

"Are you alright?" Sam asked as we got a drink from the kitchen during a break in the film. "I'm fine, I'm great," I said, nodding.

"Good, I'm so pleased you are feeling happier. I could not bear seeing you so sad any longer."

I smiled and kissed him softly. "Did you know that I think I love you?"

"No, but I do now. Did you know that I think I love you?"

"No, but I do now," I said, kissing him again. Sam was a part of me feeling better. If I didn't have Sam I would be more depressed than ever. Just the feeling of having someone who loves you, as you love them, is quite indescribable. But it was nicely indescribable.

For the rest of that evening Sam and I passed smiles across the room as everyone talked. There were times when he and I would just block out everyone else and talk to each other through smiling and eye contact. It was as if we were reading each other's minds. And to be quite honest, I think we were.

❂ ❂ ❂

About another two weeks passed with Sam and I head over heels in love ... we spent all our spare time together, seeing each other whenever we could. We would sometimes just sit together holding each other, not saying anything. It was just that feeling. Being in his arms ... I was safe ... And happy.

Then on Monday I went in for my seventh treatment. Nothing in particular happened that was different, just normal routine ... Dr Miles took some X-rays and all sorts of tests, the most tests I have had in a while.

"See you in a month Vada," Dr Miles said.

"Bye," I said, and Mum and I left and went home. I was so used to having chemotherapy that it was now just a monthly routine, it was like school. Something I had to do until it was over.

But on Thursday evening we got a phone call. It was Dr. Miles "We need you and Vada to come in, we need to talk to you," she said to my mother in a steady voice.

"When?" Mum asked.

"Tomorrow afternoon or Monday, whichever suits you best."

"Tomorrow, please."

"OK, we'll see you then."

"Bye," Mum said, putting down the phone slowly and looking puzzled.

"What is it, what is it?" I said jumping up and down.

"That was Dr Miles. She wants us to come in, she has some news for us."

"Do you think I'm OK?" I asked worried.

"I'm sure everything will be fine, I am sure it will all be fine."

That night I slept pretty badly, I was so scared. What if I was really ill and could die? What if one more treatment were not enough? I hate it, how I can be so happy and then so down. I didn't understand, and I didn't think I could wait so long to find out either.

I didn't go to school the next day, Mum said it was best to stay at home, and then we would go to the hospital later that afternoon.

I met up with my curate in the morning. He prayed with me. He prayed that everything would turn out OK. Let's just hope it will.

I cried as we prayed. The thought that God gave his only son so that all of us could live is a painful thought, but quite wonderful. There is no one like God really. I can turn to him whenever, whatever, even if it's at 3:00 in the morning. There is no one else I can turn to at that time in the morning. It's quite amazing. But sometimes I get scared, and doubt. What if he doesn't exist? But I suppose that all I can do is believe. I just hoped it would be good news that afternoon, because I needed my faith in God. Because when you go through something like I was going through, it was hard to keep believing ... I just hoped God performs a miracle, *'cause I'm not quite sure how much more of this I can take.*

I had called Sam early the same morning, just before he left for school. He'd rung the night before, and I had explained then what was going on. He seemed scared himself. But now the conversation was good. He wasn't really a believer in God, but he respected my beliefs and was prepared to listen to me talking about God. Which I thought was quite amazing. He was there which was important.

Four o'clock came, and I suddenly realised how scared I was. When I got into the car to get there I was shaking. My hands were jumping and I had butterflies in my tummy.

"Are you OK?" Mum asked.

"I'm really scared."

"Try not to worry. We are going to find out. Try to be calm." I looked up at Mum, removing a *polo* from its packet and placing it inside my mouth. My hands were slowly calming, but they were still a bit shaky. We walked down that corridor for what seemed like the hundredth time and knocked on Dr Miles' door.

"Come on in," we heard a voice say. It wasn't Dr Miles' voice, it was a man's voice. We entered. "Ah, Vada, I'm Dr Roberts, please have a seat."

Why in the world was another doctor there. I felt all confused and felt another headache coming on.

"Hi, sorry to rush you in," Dr Miles said in a nice and friendly way.

"No problem, but what's happened?" Mum asked eagerly.

"We have been studying your results from your last treatment and have got some good news for you," Dr Miles said.

"Is it shrinking?" I asked happily on hearing the news was good.

"We are quite amazed and stunned, but this can happen. We have had it checked by several other doctors, and have even had a specialist from the USA check it over," Dr Roberts went on.

"What is it, tell us?" Mum asked.

"We cannot find any trace of your tumour. It has totally disappeared." Dr Miles smiled.

"But that's impossible," I said, thinking it couldn't be true.

"It can happen, and when it does, it is nothing but a miracle. We are not joking, Vada. It is great news." I sat for a couple of seconds, stunned - but overjoyed. It now made sense why I had been feeling a bit better, my tumour had gone.

"That is wonderful! Thank you very much," Mum said, getting up and shaking hands with both doctors.

"I will need you to come back in three months' time for a check up," Dr Miles said. "But until then I won't need to see you unless you have a problem." My mouth hung open as I shook their hands and left. Mum and I walked down the corridor and at the door I stopped, realising what had happened. I was better, totally better. I started to cry.

"Vada?" Mum asked.

"I can't believe it, Mum. I am better." Mum just smiled and hugged me, really tightly.

"I know Vada, it's wonderful."

As we drove home I thought about this morning, how my curate had prayed with me.

"God certainly works fast, doesn't he?" I said to Mum. "He's performed a miracle in front of my very own eyes."

"Yes, it's amazing," she answered. "But he has always been there".

"I know, I know he has."

I'd finished the journey. I wasn't just taking a rest, but I had actually finished. There is no more uncertainty, or pain. Its over. I can't quite grasp it. It doesn't seem real. I still feel like the same old Vada, but just lighter, as if a very heavy weight has been lifted from my shoulders. It's been hard this, so hard I didn't think I was strong enough to get this far, but getting to the end, I see how much I have grown, and how much I have learnt about myself. I couldn't have been this strong without the strength